For Phoebie !,

Jake
the
Last

Colin Payne

NOV 22

A story by
Colin Payne

First published in Great Britain as a softback original in 2022

Copyright © Colin Payne

The moral right of this author has been asserted.

Editing, design, typesetting and publishing by UK Book Publishing

www.ukbookpublishing.com

ISBN: 978-1-915338-12-9

For all those who may, one day,
actually give a damn...

Acknowledgements and Thanks

I want to thank **Anders (Andy) Payne** for his patience. It must have been hard taking questions from the least bush savvy of all his male relatives. Besides, there's something unexplainably wonderful about flying 500ft above Tsava sitting next to the helicopter pilot that you once bounced on your knee!

Godknows Masiri the Zimbabwean artist who painted the amazing front cover. An enormous talent. He lives in Harare, Zimbabwe. Ndinotenda zvikuru, Masiri!

John W. W. Payne is my older brother. Together with my younger brother Ed, and my Dad, they taught me everything I needed to know to get to the next sunrise. John has been my sounding board on all matters beyond my laptop keyboard. Thanks, Johnny!

I must also thank **Graham Boynton and Ruben (Rob) Zipper.** My two home town friends for giving me an ending to the story whilst we were having lunch at Il Conte in Soho.

Br. Mark Hallissey (R.I.P) He believed in me when others didn't.

Angus Bryce Hyland-Smith. I call him Smithy. It's quicker. Over a glass or two of good Scotch whisky, we talked about farming, friendship, war, music and Jake the black rhinoceros. Cheers, Smithy!

Patricia O'Sullivan is a choir mistress and accomplished author. She is also very patient.

Simon Phiri, an artist who trained at Mzilikazi Art Centre in Bulawayo. Simon drew the poachers on the back cover. He also did the wildlife drawings throughout this book. Simon is a gentle man. Ngiyabonga kakhulu, Phiri!

Travis Sletcher and I are the best of friends and have been for 45 years. He shuttled Simon's artwork from KwaZulu Natal to Hertfordshire and the metropolitan county of Tyne and Wear. He is very funny and brutally honest. It's a pity about his legs, though.

Dianne V. Payne. She agreed to marry me. Such courage! My children and grandchildren who told me to, "please read Jake for us, Pop. Please!". They said it was their favourite bedtime story. Who loves ya?

I would also like to thank **Ruth** and **Jay** at **UK Book Publishing** for their help, advice and confidence.

Jake the Last

You could be forgiven for thinking that Jake was always sad. Those round shoulders, drooping forehead, chin scraping the ground and his eyes glazed over as though he had cried all his tears out. But, you'd be wrong. Beneath the caricature of sadness lay a sense of humour drier than his thick folds of armour-like skin.

"Battle ship grey!" he mused. "Who thought of that? If anything, it should be *rhinoceros* grey. We've been around a lot longer than battle ships. Mind you, I'm not sure the we-were-here-first rule applies anymore."

He munched away at the fresh leaves and green twigs. His feet moving only to shift him towards the next mouthful. "Then," he thought, "although all rhinoceroses are grey, it was decided that those with the flat lip should be called white. Those with the hook-lip, like me, should be called black. Well, they got that completely wrong, too. What they actually meant to say was, 'wide' lipped rhinoceros. In time, that was lost in translation and became 'white' lipped rhinoceros. Finally, born of laziness and a quest to patronize the gods of shortcuts, it's been reduced to Black Rhino and White Rhino. It would seem that everything makes more sense, to them, if it's either black or white. Which is really quite odd," thought Jake, "because so little on this amazing planet is neither black nor white. Hmmm... a strange lot, this animal called human. Very strange indeed."

Jake loved it out here on the savannah. Under blue skies on green grass, he walked, he ate, he drank. Unhurried, he browsed, he listened, he breathed in the perfumes, the smells, the stink and the aroma of complete freedom. The Serengeti was his home. It covered twelve thousand square miles. It was bigger than Hawaii, three times larger than Jamaica, one and a half times bigger than Israel. Even its name means The Vast Plain. It is believed that the habitat has remained unchanged for millions of years!

"Oh, yes," thought Jake. "This is my home. I was born here. I was raised here by my mother. This is where I belong!"

Jake stopped. His ears flicked independently of each other. He lifted his huge head and tested the savannah breeze. All clear. Well, almost. A vaguely familiar smell tickled his large oval nostrils.

He stood still. Perfectly still.

"I'm Jake. You're entering my space and you need a very good reason for being here."

He paused.

"Step forward, step forward... slowly," added Jake threateningly. "Show yourself."

Now, when two full grown black male rhinos square up to each other, it's as if the very air holds its breath.

"It's me, Jake. It's Reuben."

More silence.

"Can we talk?"

They fell into step, side by side. From the back, they looked like two old men in baggy, grey flannel trousers shuffling along the Eastbourne Pier. They walked slowly, almost a stroll. Their gait suited their size, bulk and shape. It also hinted at their power and strength. The horn looked threatening and somewhat out of place. Rhinoceros are herbivores. They don't eat meat and do not kill to eat.

"So, what's new, Reuben?" began Jake, starting to relax a little.

"It's a new day, Jake. A never-been-used-before day and ours to do with it as we please. That's what's new today and isn't that exactly how we like it?" replied Reuben, sounding upbeat.

"Oh yes. There's a certain charm in things being the same most of the time, Reuben. It gives one something to rely on. Something to lean against. Something one can trust."

"That's true, Jake." Reuben paused. "Take us, for example, 350 million years later we're still pretty much the same in appearance."

Jake stood about 5ft at the shoulder. He measured just over 12ft from nose to tail and weighed just under 4000 lbs. Jake was big. Reuben, on the other hand, looked a little bit smaller because his horn was shorter. Reuben also weighed around 4000 lbs and was probably a shade under 5ft at the shoulder. His horn was nearly 20 inches long. Whereas, Jake's horn was a whopping 31 inches long!

They stopped in the shade of a big candelabra tree. A large, spiny, succulent tree with all the branches growing from a single trunk.

It looks very much like a cluster of candles. Hence, the name candelabra. In the spring, it randomly sprouts beautiful bright yellow flowers. However, the milky sap which flows when the tree is nicked or cut, is quite dangerous to humans. It can cause blindness if it gets into the eyes and... it has a burning and stinging sensation if it gets onto human skin. It doesn't bother black rhinoceroses.

"Things around us have really changed a lot, though," began Reuben, "and that's what I want to talk to you about."

He went on, "Did you hear about that Cecil the Lion business in Zimbabwe?"

"I did. Avril told me. What is all the fuss about? I don't quite follow. It's not as though Cecil was the very last male lion. Was he?"

Jake didn't wait for an answer. "It's important to remember that it is a business, Reuben." He paused. "Let me explain."

The pair of them eased their way out of the shade, and Jake continued, "The man in charge gets the money, the American dentist kills the King of the Beasts and... the Internet holds a requiem. It's that simple, Reuben." They stopped to eat some more.

"Don't misunderstand me, Reuben, it's a sad state of affairs and I am as upset and appalled as the rest of the world and... at the risk of sounding shallow or disinterested, that's just the way it is, my friend. Just the way it is."

They trudged lazily forward.

"Hmmm... so, are you saying, that in today's money, thirty pieces of silver is worth $35,000 US dollars?"

"No, Reuben. Don't put words in my mouth," countered Jake. "What I *am* saying is this. On the very same day that Cecil the Lion was killed in Zimbabwe, local subsistent farmers killed a cheetah barely a mile from where we are right now."

"Is that so?" Reuben enthused. "Just a mile from here? What happened?"

"The cheetah," continued Jake, "an old female, was seen trying to force her way into the farmer's keep. The bleating goats raised the alarm and the farmer, his wife, two sons and daughter rushed to the keep."

"Well," added Reuben, "they would protect their food and livestock, wouldn't they?"

Jake continued, "In the hope that the cheetah might lose interest and go elsewhere for her meal, the family teased, frightened and confused her by banging their cooking pots together and yelling at the tops of their voices! Then, in her panic and attempts to escape, the cheetah got straddled atop the crude fence, lost her balance and crashed to the ground, dragging the fence with her."

"Then what happened, Jake?" asked Reuben, getting excited.

"Well, the goats and chickens scattered. The farmer's eldest son ran back to the hut and returned with the spear. Of course, the more the cheetah struggled, the more she became entangled in the broken-down fence. The shouting and pot banging family continued making a din. Then, bewildered, exhausted and held tight in the tangled fence, the cheetah collapsed onto her side. Her breathing was fast and noisy."

Jake paused as if the very telling of the tale had tired him out, as well.

"With her side fully exposed, the farmer's son rushed in and thrust the spear deep into the old cheetah's chest and retreated quickly to watch the poison do its work. She tried to free the spear by bringing her hind legs up to her chest and pawing away at the spear shaft. Ironically, the fastest animal on this planet was held tight in the wire. The poison-tipped spear sticking awkwardly out of her chest." Respectfully, Jake stopped for a moment and allowed the telling of the horror to form a picture in their minds.

"Finally," said Jake, "after nearly three hours of unspeakable agony, the cheetah died..."

Silence.

Then slowly, quietly and deliberately, he turned to Reuben and asked, "Did *that* go viral on the Internet?"

"No," answered Reuben.

"Do you know why it didn't make cyberspace headlines?" probed Jake.

"Well... a cheetah taking a goat for her dinner and a farmer defending his livestock is not a news story, Reuben. It's what the cheetah does and it's what the farmer does. It is life and it is death. Side by side, where they've always been," explained Jake.

They shuffled along in silence. Each deep in their own thoughts.

"Now, here's the real tragedy," continued Jake slowly, "elephants, lions and rhinoceroses are just the headlines. The bigger story is the human-wildlife conflict. A conflict fuelled by a growing population needing more land and more resources to sustain them. The ultimate casualty of this conflict will be the environment."

"Are you following this, Reuben? It's not who or what. No. It's where, why and how."

"I hear you, Jake. Only, you're telling me something I already know."

The Poachers

Issa Duale was not a native of the Serengeti. He was a poacher. His homeland was Somalia, more than 500 miles to the northeast. However, Issa knew this part of the Serengeti very well. He had come here many times to kill rhinoceroses. He shot them, hacked off their horns and fled. Issa is 5ft 9ins tall and slightly built. You could even say he was quite skinny. He wasn't as dark-skinned as the local Masai tribesmen so his eyes didn't look as bright, but those eyes seemed to be constantly shifting from left to right.

Issa could run fast for long periods of time. He could shoot quite well. Not as well as the game rangers but well enough to do what he had come to do. Over the years he had got better.

Haassan Ahmed was also a Somali. A lifelong friend of Issa and also a poacher. He was a little bit bigger than Issa. He did not shoot rhinoceros nor elephant. No, he hacked the horns and tusks from animals that

Issa shot. He was strong. You could see the muscle and sinew in his physique.

Issa was an excellent tracker. Not only on the spoor but also understanding the wind, the sun's shadows and the rhino's habits. Issa also knew his own capabilities and his limits. He understood that silence, stealth, water and rest were just as important to hunting as his rifle and ammunition.

Suddenly Issa raised his hand. They stopped. Issa could smell droppings. Rhino droppings. Male rhino droppings. They followed the scent. After a few minutes the smell was very strong and looking down, Issa saw the huge pile of poo to which the smell in his nose had been guiding him. He put his index finger into the large pile, removed it and placed it gently against his cheek. "Hmmm... still warm. We're getting closer."

Unaware of the poachers, the two rhinoceroses strolled on. Stopping and stooping to munch on the grasses and pulling at roots and shoots so abundant on the grassland floor. Tearing and ripping at the smaller saplings and shrubs. There always seemed to be plenty to eat and enough water to drink out here on the grassy plains of East Africa. As the sun rose higher, the sky paled and the air got hot. Jake and Reuben edged their way into the trees for some shade to cool down and rest.

Reuben smiled and gently shook his head. "You have obviously spent a lot of time mulling over this environment business, Jake. Keep on thinking about it. That's what you're good at and why I wanted to talk with you."

"Is that so?" asked Jake in a theatrically patronizing sort of way. "Then, if I'm so good at thinking, pray tell, dear friend, what are *you* good at?"

"Listening, Jake. Listening and smelling. That's what I'm really good at and... right now, I hear trouble and smell danger!"

Bang! Bang! Bang! It came from behind. They had heard that sound before. The two of them reacted quickly and started to run. Jake nudged Reuben left as they crashed into the thicket of thorny trees. Reuben veered away and smashed his own pathway to who knows where. His short legs strained as they forced his 4000 lb body forward. Keep going forward. Don't look back. Don't give them a bigger target. Keep going forward. The future is always in front of you.

Jake barged and shoved his way through trees young and old. He bounced off the bigger and harder ones and trampled the lesser and the fallen. Some branches and saplings got all tangled up in his short powerful legs but none, not one, stopped him from going ever forward. He could hear his breath above the crack of the rifle shots and the whine of the bullets as they whizzed ever nearer.

Always onwards, always forward. Quite suddenly, his snorting breath was the only sound he could hear. He thought his heart might explode in his deep chest as he snatched at the air for breath. Had the shooting stopped? Jake stopped. Listened. His breath grew louder and louder in the eerie silence. The whole of the Serengeti seemed to be listening. Waiting. This false tranquillity. This pregnant calm...

...Thump! Thump! Thump! The dull sound of the axe beat its way into the silence. It felt as though the ground was shaking as it bashed and battered Reuben's face. Even the grass seemed to shrink in horror. The animal kingdom bawled its pain into the echo. Jake tossed his head from side to side, trying desperately to rid his ears of the axe's deathly drumbeat. He snorted; he stamped his front feet. He charged his anger into a nearby granite boulder.

He charged again, and again and again. Exhausted, Jake toppled forward. His tired front legs folded under him. Dust billowed out as his large body thumped onto the ground. Through his burning breath, he mumbled, "Reuben, Reuben, Reuben..."

What next?

Jake wasn't sure how long he had lain there. It must've been quite a while because he felt heavy, lumpy, tired and sore.

"Jake! Jake! Are you OK? What happened?"

He could hear Avril but he wasn't sure if he was listening or, just remembering.

Avril is a red-billed oxpecker. An unusual bird in many ways and probably most well-known for her peculiar and often disgusting diet. She eats ticks and other bugs and parasites that she plucks from the many large animals of Africa. Giraffe, buffalo, impala, rhinoceros and zebra are all on her list of favourite eating places. If not for her signature red bill, Avi is a somewhat nondescript greyish brown pigeon-sized bird. Her red eyes are surrounded by yellow eye-rings. These are, in fact, the un-feathered skin around the eye. Very pretty. Her short energetic flying style from a quick launch takes her from animal to animal and back to her nest. For the benefit of all, Avi's alarm call announces that danger is approaching.

"Humph," Jake snorted himself awake. He could feel Avril doing the morning tidy as she picked and pecked in his left ear. He twitched and flicked her away. She hopped back and almost in the same movement returned to the smorgasbord in Jake's other ear.

"Not now, Avril!" he grumbled. "Come back later."

"No," protested Avril. "I've been looking everywhere for you and because of it, my schedule is a complete shambles. Everyone's hiding out, and poachers or not, I have my work to finish and family to feed." Peck, pull, peck, peck, pull. Avril hopped up onto his back and fluttered her way into his ears again.

"So, Jake, while I'm about my business, tell me what happened."

"Whatever do you mean?" muttered Jake. Half asleep, half awake and completely confused.

"Are you serious? You don't know?!" the oxpecker asked in amazement.

"Avril!" snorted the awakening rhino. "I'm beginning to lose my patience." Jake was getting agitated with the oxpecker. He continued through clenched teeth. "I don't know what you're talking about or, I don't remember whatever it is you're talking about. Either way, if you have something to say that you think I might find important, start talking! Start talking before I go from being just-got-up-grumpy to downright intolerable!" Jake was yelling.

"Reuben is dead. Shot. De-horned and left to stink." Avril spoke clearly and slowly. She had no intention of repeating it.

"Oh no!" The reminder squeezed his heart. He tried to stand up but stumbled, rocked back and forth, then fell back against the granite boulder. He was dizzy. He leaned against the boulder as his balance slowly returned and his breathing became more regular. Then, after what seemed like a whole dry season, Jake stood up and began to speak. "I was with him, Avi," Jake began quietly, "when the shooting started, we split up. I heard the shooting. It was being sprayed all over the place.

"I just kept running till I couldn't go on. Then, I heard the sickening sound of the axe and, and... I smashed into this rock. I just wanted to chase that thumping noise out of my ears." He turned slowly towards the bird. "I wanted to die, Avi." He stalled. "Right now?" He stalled again. "I still do."

"I know, Jake. I know." Avril the red-billed oxpecker tried to offer some understanding and comfort. If she could have, she would've hugged him. It's a sad thing to see strength, power and courage reduced to weeping.

"He was my friend, Avi," he began slowly. "For as long as I can remember, he was my friend. Come to think of it, they are all my friends." Jake paused to collect himself. "True, we weren't in each other's pockets. We are Diceros Bicornis Rhinoceros; we don't do that sort of thing. Our mothers raised us along with other calves. Then, after about three years or so, we moved off. I never knew and I don't think I ever met my father. None of us did. In an odd sort of way, you might say we were born to be orphans." He stopped speaking and thought about what he had just said.

"My friendship with Reuben and, for that matter, the rest of the animal kingdom is based on respect, common understanding and space. Yes, Reuben and I have had our differences but that only confirmed what we are... black rhinoceros." He let his words hang on the edge of silence then, drawing a deep breath, continued in his words-of-wisdom tone.

"Let me tell you something, Avi. When you start running out of friends, you start running out of good reasons to carry on. Friends and family are what makes the first rains worth waiting for. Friends tell you when the fire's coming. Friends laugh at the young ones in a way that makes the youngsters feel welcome and safe. Friends listen." He paused to allow his words to make sense.

"I'll tell you something else, Avi. The only time you even *think* about dying is when a friend or family member passes. Up until then, you think about water, food, yesterday, shade, tomorrow, mud, sleep but... when you've got friends," Jake continued, "sometimes, you don't think about anything at all. Do you know why that is? Do you know why you don't think about anything at all, Avi? I'll tell you why," Jake went on, "you don't think about anything at all because you're too busy laughing. That's right, Avi! Just too busy laughing..." He tailed off.

Through the silence there came truth. Jake's truth. Swaddled in sadness, sorrow and grief. He was a pitiful sight. The identifying hooked lip was torn, his iconic horn was grazed and chipped on the point. His head hung on his powerful neck as though the slightest bump might cause it to fall off. Sadness and grief have a way of making faces look heavy. So heavy that they seem to grow longer and in danger of slipping away altogether.

After a long and respectable silence, Avi spoke up.

"So, what are you going to do, Jake?" Before he could answer she re-shaped her question. "What do you *want* to do?"

"I don't know, Avi. I really don't know." He went on, "I need time to think about this."

"Well, factor this into your thoughts..." said Avril. "Asher the bull elephant, says you're doomed. All rhinoceroses, and he did say all. Males, female, black, white and the calves. I mean all rhinoceroses are doomed! Shot to extinction. Shot into hell."

"Oh! That's rich." Jake perked up at the very mention of Asher. "That's really rich!" he continued, with sarcasm dripping from every word. "Extinction! Shot to extinction! Is that what he said? Well, coming from a bull elephant with seven foot of prime ivory sat either side of his extraordinary long nose. Oh! This is priceless!" ridiculed Jake. "Doesn't he understand that if *we* go, his lot will be next? In fact, they may even go first!" Then with fawned sympathy, he added, "But with his poor eyesight I guess he can't see that."

"I'm not sure that you should bring poor eyesight into your assessment of Asher's shortcomings, Jake. There are those who might suggest that it's a perfect case of the pot calling the kettle black or, white or, battleship grey."

Jake could feel his face relaxing, and he wanted to smile at Avi's razor-sharp wit but he winced as he felt the pain of his swollen and cut lip. He was hungry and the lip, painful or not, had work to do. He started to walk slowly, pausing to eat until his lip didn't bother him.

"Have you considered taking that de-horning option, Jake? Seems to be working in the southern regions," offered the red billed oxpecker in a sustained effort to keep the conversation from slipping backwards.

"Who told you that?"

"Harvey told me."

"Harvey?! Harvey the hyena? Harvey?!!" Jake repeated. "That lying son-of-a-bitch wouldn't know the truth if it was served up crawling in maggots. Hyenas don't do truth. They lie to their mothers the day after they're born. It's Mother Nature's trade-off, Avi. She gives the hyena the strongest jaws in the kingdom and then takes away their honesty. Can you seriously believe anything that smells that bad, feeds on rotting corpses and laughs at the sight of death?"

"Stop it! Jake. That's harsh. Harvey deals in the truth. Death *is* the truth. The ultimate truth." It was Avi's turn to sprout some philosophy. She continued, "Furthermore... between Harvey and his gang and Valentine and her band of vultures, I believe they do an extraordinary job. If you want proof, tell me, when did you last hear of anyone getting sick around here?! Jeez, Jake. We've all got a job to do. We are a perfect society and your moody criticism is uncalled for!" If Avi had hands, they'd have been on her hips. She was angry.

The black rhino was taken aback at the oxpecker's rebuke.

"You're right, Avi," apologized Jake. "I was bang out of order. Somebody has to take out the rubbish. I'm sorry."

"I should think so, too," said Avi, knowing the importance of having the last word. "Now... can we please return to this de-horning option?"

"It's not for me, Avi. The horn is who and what I am. A rhinoceros without a horn is the same as a leopard without spots, or a zebra without stripes, an elephant without a trunk. Furthermore, when the poachers are tracking, they don't know if we've been de-horned or not. When they're close enough to see for themselves, they shoot anyway. They don't want to be wasting any more time tracking hornless rhinoceros. No, Avi! The horn goes, I go."

"Well you hit the nail right on the head, Jake. No rhino, no horn. No horn, no rhino."

Silence entered the conversation as the sounds of the savannah trickled into their space. The scratching of the beetles, the giggles and hiccups coming from the grass and the chirps and shrills in the air overhead. There is always so much going on. Spiders building webs, beetles scurrying around droppings, flies buzzing around almost everything and birds of all shapes, sizes and colours go to-ing and fro-ing about their business.

Suddenly and very quietly, Jake said, "Take me to him, Avi. Take me to Reuben."

The oxpecker skipped along his back and hopped up to his ear.

"What?" Avi exclaimed. "Jake. I don't think this a good idea. The poachers might still be around. Besides, you won't even recognize him. Reuben is not there. It's just a stinking, rotting carcass attracting all the usual eaters of decaying meat. It's ugly, Jake."

"Ugly? I'm ugly, Avi. Rhinos are ugly. We're 350 million years in the making and we're still ugly! If we were panda bears, baby seals, lion cubs or lambs, we'd be on the Disney Channel, birthday cards and corporate stationery. But... we're not. Ugly doesn't scare me, Avi. Take me to Reuben."

"Jake. Think about this. Please..."

"I have thought about it. You asked me what I wanted to do. I want to see Reuben."

The Clearing

As he strode into the clearing – a new, freshly trodden clearing – every living creature turned to look at Jake. Like school children caught doing something they shouldn't, they began to look for support among those next to them. Nervous eyes darted around the clearing, looking for leadership, hoping for leadership. Backing away from their meal and flicking anxious glances towards Jake. The silence hung as heavy as the sweet smell of death.

"Sorry, Jake," lied Harvey. "Sorry for your loss," Harvey lied again.

"It's OK," Jake half replied, ignoring Harvey's false apology, "just give me a few moments and then you can all go back to doing what you do."

The air in the clearing softened as hyena, vultures, flies, spiders and beetles relaxed under the comfort of Jake's absolution. They drew back as the rhino, with Avril on his shoulder, approached the remains of his dear friend.

At first, Jake did not fully understand what he was looking at. He had seen carcasses before, of course, and even with his poor eyesight he could see when it was a zebra, a wildebeest or Thomson's gazelle. But this was strange. He could not reconcile his memory of Reuben to what lay in front of him. It was grotesque. Jake felt as though everything around him was spinning. He blinked. He blinked again, hoping that the spinning would stop. He was dizzy.

"Jake. Let's go," whispered Avril. "Come along Jake, this isn't doing any of us any good. Jake!" She tried to shake him from his trance.

The spinning stopped. Without the horn, it was hard for Jake to make out Reuben's head from his tail. The haste with which the horn had been hacked and ripped from him was obvious. The cavity in his face, where his horn had once been, lay bare and a slash of white bone peeped through the darkening blood. Reuben's once proud head was littered with dust that mixed with the blood to form muddy scabs. His lips were parted and distorted in anguish. Those slow eyes pulled wide in terror.

It occurred to Jake that Reuben could have still been alive when the axe had started to hack his rhinoceros-ness from him. Deep within his fear, instinct and strength, Reuben had fought for his life. Aiming his horn at nothing and everything. Then, Issa the poacher had fired into his ear. Again and again and again.

Jake's shock began to subside. He steadied himself. He could feel the anger welling up inside him. He stood back, stomped his feet and tossed his head. Avril took off. He grunted, slowly lowered his head and then, using his horn to help him focus, he glared at all who had now gathered on the edge of the clearing. The wildebeest, the zebra, the giraffe and buffalo were all there. Baboons sat on their haunches and the lions stood still. In the shadow, he thought he saw Asher the bull elephant. Poor eyesight and all, he scanned the ringside once more. It *was* Asher.

"Come out of the shadow, oh grey wise one with long nose, long memory, sought after ivory and sticky-out ears! Come and look!" Jake began mockingly. "Come and see what your 'such-is-life attitude' has got us."

The gathering inched backwards half expecting a fight.

"You, Asher. You are next. Then Hagar the lioness, then Sherman the Buffalo and then Kelvin and the wild dogs. So it goes, until the food chain feeds of itself. Out of order, out of time and out of hope."

The bull elephant lifted his head. Flapped his ears challenging Jake to continue.

"The best you can expect, Asher, is a Remembrance Day! That's right, January 21st is World Elephant Day!" began Jake in his best Barnum and Bailey ringmaster's voice. "They shake their tins and they purge their consciences with small change. Pledging that this tragedy must never happen again. Then... when it does, they just hold another Remembrance Day. Simple as that. They just re-label the tins from elephants to Syrian refugees!" Jake paused for effect.

"Is that what you want, Asher? Do you want to be a tragedy?" Asher backed deeper into the shadows.

"Mark my words," Jake continued, "if you leave it to them, that is precisely what you will become. Yes sir! Just another tragedy in their long line of this-must-never-happen-again tragedies."

The collective silence seemed to suggest that Jake was making sense to all those gathered at the clearing.

"It's what they do, Asher. Don't you understand?" pleaded Jake. "They kill the unborn, they violate their young, and they attack and ridicule every variation of their own kind. They are without tolerance, understanding or patience." He waited, letting it sink in.

"Save the Rhino, they cry. What?! Save the Rhino! Don't make me laugh. They can't even save themselves! They cannot save themselves, from themselves," emphasized Jake.

"Listen to me," he continued. The gathering leaned forward, straining so as not to miss a word. "Thousands of years ago, a faceless, invisible God granted Man dominium over everything that has the breath of life. Well, let me tell you this," he went on, "if something invisible ever offers you dominium over anything, don't accept! Do not accept unless you acknowledge that the rule of dominium is love, respect, kindness and the tireless pursuit of understanding."

"Oh! and while I still have your attention," he paused and then staring straight at Asher, he continued, "whatever will be, will be... is bullshit!"

Then, through the strength of his character and the depths of his conviction, he stared at Reuben's carcass and added, "Whatever will be, will be...if you let it."

The ground trembled as he turned to leave the clearing. He stopped, looked back and said, "Carry on, Harvey. Carry on, all of you. Carry on doing what you do but," he interrupted himself, "not as though nothing has happened, but rather that something is about to!"

The silence was deafening.

Time

J ake peered into the soft light of the morning. All was calm. There were no strange smells, no grass fires. Jake's acute hearing caught the peaceful repetitive melody of the morning's chorus. There wasn't the harsh chatter of the vervet monkey nor the ruckus barking of baboons. Those same baboons become loud when foraging for food before returning to their granite kopje hideaway.

"That was quite some speech you gave over Reuben's carcass last night, Jake!" offered Avril as she fluttered and hopped her way along his spine. "The whole place is talking about it. Except Asher, of course. Seems you managed to get right up his nose and... we all know that takes some doing." Avril giggled.

"Well, maybe I was a little over the top, Avi. Emotion has a way of blurring the edges of truth. However, I meant what I said. Naturally, there will be those who will edit out the bits they don't like, don't believe or don't understand. Nonetheless, just as long as they're talking about what they heard, there might be a chance that some good will come out of it."

"So... what are you going to do, Jake?" enquired the ever-inquisitive oxpecker.

"Well," paused the rhino, "I believe I'm going to take some time to think about that, Avi and... if it's all the same to you, I am going to need some time alone."

"Time alone?" repeated Avi, laughing. "How much more time can you actually spend alone to need to spend *more* time alone? Really, Jake! If 'time alone' was an Olympic sport, you'd scoop the bronze, silver and the gold medals!"

Jake chortled at Avi's wit and wisdom. "You know what I mean, somewhere quiet and peaceful. A place where I can hear myself eat. A place where thinking is timeless and thoughts are like drops of rain. Each one welcome, precious and full of hope."

"Very well, I think I understand." She paused. "You want to be left alone. Left alone so that you can make a plan?" Avi's words were clear and unhurried. She bobbed along and settled in the gap between Jake's big horn and the lesser one. Surprisingly, and for a bird with a rather questionable diet, her head was quite pretty. The tell-tale red beak set off against a muddy greyish face with beautiful red eyes set in a reddish orange iris surrounded by a bright yellow ring. She continued.

"You want to make a plan," Avi repeated.

"Correct," answered Jake.

"Very well," confirmed Avi. "I shall leave you alone. I shall leave you alone on condition that, firstly, you tell me exactly where you intend to go, and secondly... no mud baths!" She flapped onto the top of the lesser horn. "I mean it, Jake," she warned, "if you take a wallow, you may as well leave your name and address. You will just be making it easier for these horn hunting bandits to find you. Remember, they have seen you. They know your whereabouts and they want this horn." She hopped to the side and pecked at the huge perfectly shaped horn that identified and distinguished the rhinoceros from all other animals.

The seriousness of Avi's terms and conditions was obvious.

"OK Avi," conceded Jake, "I understand."

"So, where exactly, are you going, Jake?" pressed the oxpecker.

"OK, I shall be around that small kopjie by the donga where Aileen and Kelvin used to live."

"Aileen and Kelvin?"

"You know Aileen and Kelvin. The wild dogs?" explained Jake.

"Of course," replied Avi, surprised at her forgetfulness.

"All right. Just one more thing, Jake."

"Hmmm... how is it that I knew there would be more," muttered the Black Rhino.

"Five nights. That's all you have, Jake. Five nights and then... I'll tell the world where you are and you can wave peace and quiet goodbye!"

"Come on, Avi," pleaded Jake. "What if I find I need more time?"

"You don't need any more time!" Avi protested. "You have your plan half-baked already. Besides, if you're not seen around and about, someone's going to start talking. Five nights, Jake or, I'll spread your whereabouts so quickly, it'll make the news about Cecil the Lion look like four lines in the obituaries column. You know I can do it, Jake," Avril warned. "One word from me and every oxpecker on the savannah will pass it on to everything that walks, swims, crawls and flies. Once the savannah knows, our whole world knows." She stopped. "Do you understand me, Jake?"

He nodded, turned slowly and walked quietly into the long grass and seemed to melt into his surroundings. For all intents and purposes, Jake had disappeared.

Shooting the Breeze

It was evening, the light was fading quickly and the air was starting to cool.

Nyx was lapping gently from the stream. Leopards never seem to look at the water when they drink. Their eyes appear to be scanning the opposite bank. Slurp, slurp, slurp. Then, still in the crouch position, she raised her head slightly and looked upstream and slowly downstream. Slurp, slurp, slurp.

From the opposite bank, Sherman was watching her. Then easing forward, he also began to drink. Buffalo are noisy when they drink. Their long tongues are always busy. Firstly, it's in the water. Then, back in their mouths and then, reaching out and upwards to wash their snouts.

The black buffalo is powerful and, seemingly, short tempered. That makes them dangerous. Their horns are quite comical and look out of place, almost like the turned-up brim of the hat of a Swiss milk maid.

Sherman inched his front legs into the stream and began to drink. Slurp, slurp. slurp.

Suddenly, on the opposite bank and 30 feet upstream from Nyx the leopard, Hagar the lioness tip-toed up to the water's edge and began the slurp, slurp, slurp like the leopard. Hagar was bigger than Nyx and although they were both considered big cats, the lioness was noticeably larger in every respect.

Elephants seem to struggle to do anything quietly. Eating, drinking, walking or mating, all seem to be very loud activities. Why should they be quiet? Standing 13 feet at the shoulder and weighing as much as 14000 lbs, the African elephants are the largest land mammal on the planet. Their only threat comes from humans.

Asher the bull elephant strode out from the trees and placed his two front feet in the stream. He then dipped his trunk into the cool water, snorted up a little of the refreshing liquid and promptly sprayed it into his mouth. No slurping required.

"What really sickens me," began Sherman, "is if you wave enough money around, someone will find a way, no matter how despicable, of helping you to part with it."

"Very true," confirmed Asher.

"King of the Jungle? I don't think so," said Sherman, dipping his head and acknowledging Hagar on the opposite bank. "Lions are the Sultans of the Savannah."

Asher nodded. "It's like you've always said, Sherman. They just make it up as they go along." The buffalo stepped forward into the stream and his tongue began the water-to-mouth-to-snout journey. Then he lifted his head and continued.

"Take that Big Five thing, for example. What is that all about and... how do you make it *in* to the big five, exactly?"

Nyx pulled back from the water's edge. She stretched out of the crouch position and stared straight at Asher, waiting for his answer to Sherman's question.

"Don't you remember how upset Mildred was when she heard that hippos were not included?" asked Asher. "Now, I ask you, how big does one have to be, for goodness sake?" He dipped his trunk back into the water.

"We're in the Big Five because they think we're the five hardest animals to kill," whispered the leopard.

"Yes," added Hagar the lioness. "How come the cheetah isn't in the Big Five? I mean, it has to be quite hard to kill the fastest animal in the world?"

"Hagar is right," confirmed Sherman. "And when I come to think about it, being in their Big Five carries no perks, whatsoever!"

"If anything," chipped in Hagar, "it is a crazy distorted image of Africa."

"And what is more," added the leopard quietly, "we get a superstar status which only raises our value in the killing fields."

"OK, look at it this way, then. If all the elephants are wiped out – sorry about that, Asher – do we then have the Big Four?" offered Sherman the buffalo.

"Perhaps they should have a promotion and relegation rule," added Nyx the leopard. "Elephants relegated, and the giraffe and zebra will have a run off to see who is promoted?" They all began to chuckle at the silliness of their banter.

Aah, sundowners. Slurp, slurp, slurp. You've got to laugh.

"You're right, Sherman, they haven't got a clue. Don't you just love it when they warn each other that 'it's a jungle out there'! Who are they kidding? They wouldn't know the jungle from a timber yard if it wasn't on TV. In fact, the more I think about it, they don't really know much about anything!" added Hagar the Lioness.

"Hmmm... I wouldn't go that far," corrected Nyx, "they certainly know all there is to know about killing. They are the best in the world at it. Snares, rifles, bows and arrows, traps, spears. You name it, they use it."

"It's what they do, my friends. It's what they have always done. Killing? Humph... you might say, that they were born for it," concluded Asher.

When Sherman the buffalo looked up, he was alone. "Why wasn't Jake with us this evening?" he asked himself.

Alone?

Jake chomped mouthful after mouthful of the young Acacia shoots. They were good. The tiny green leaves and their stems were full of flavour, and that reminded Jake of the exceptional rains that the Serengeti and Ngorongoro areas had received last year.

He had dim memories of browsing for food with his mother in the west of Ngorongoro many years ago. Reuben and he had enjoyed playing around together. Scattering the flocks of guinea fowl with their mock charges, or harassing the feeding groups of gazelles. Their short legs gave them a rocking horse motion as they darted here and there. A comical innocence.

He also remembered the growing up part and how he came to enjoy his own company. He wasn't lonely. He just understood that that's what rhinos did. They simply went about their own business not interfering with anyone or anything. Until they were provoked or threatened. Then... the bulk, the power, and the horn combined to protect him.

"Why would anyone want to change this," he thought to himself. "This *is* the Garden of Eden. Everything works. Everything in it knows its place, its purpose and loves it."

Jake stood still. The sun was climbing higher and it was very hot. He had found a young Marula tree, which only just provided sufficient shade for the bulk of a mature male Black Rhinoceros. The young tree had already started to drop its leaves and its shade was patchy. This suited Jake's needs, as the dappled shade was cooling and also helped to camouflage him.

A short while before, Jake had heard the distant call of a Grey Lourie or, as they were commonly called, the Go-away Bird. The bird's signature tune put Jake on alert. His nostrils flared and his ears twitched and flicked, searching for signs of the intruder that had triggered the Go-away call. A small group of Coqui Francolin passed close by. Their relaxed feeding indicated to Jake that all was well.

He heard something. He heard it again. It sounded like stealth trying not to be clumsy. Then he heard a deep dry cough and almost at the same time the ammonia-like smell of cat's pee. Big cat's pee!

"Lion," Jake whispered. Then, standing bold, he called out, "I am Jake the Black Rhino. I mean no harm. Come out. Let me see you."

The silence began to tremble as leaves were brushed aside and young low branches flicked out of the way. The breathing was short with the rasp of old age.

"Hello Jake, what are you doing out here?"

"I might ask you the same question," replied Jake. "Come closer, let me get a better look at you."

"It's me, Charlemagne. Ex-King of the Jungle, black-maned, man-eating lion. Simba!'

Jake stared at him. The lion was skinny. He was scarred across his nose and also across his bony shoulders. He was a lot smaller than the last time they had met. His once proud mane was matted, and scraggly. Bits of it were missing as were a couple of teeth.

"Good heavens, Charlie, you look awful. What happened?"

The lion seemed to shrink further under the discomfort of the question.

"Life, Jake. That's what happened. Life."

"I don't understand, Charlie. What does that mean? Life?"

Charlie drew a deep sigh which triggered a dry cough. He licked his muzzle, paused, then began to speak.

"The young lions take over, Jake. It's what they do. Oh, you can be sure that I resisted. These scars are proof of that," said Charlie. "I resisted for as long as I could, but when my experience was no match for their strength or desire, I moved on. I had to. You know how it goes, Jake."

"Sorry to hear that, Charlie."

"Don't be," cut in the lion, "it's the order of things or, as they say, the Law of the Jungle."

"What? Please don't tell me that you buy that 'law of the jungle' stuff?"

"No Jake, I was being sarcastic," replied the lion. "I'm allowed to be sarcastic in my old age. However," he continued, "I do believe in, and understand, the laws of nature."

"Which are?" questioned Jake.

"Well... I have always known that I would go from having my meals caught for me to having to fend for myself," said Charlie as he lay down and crouched in that famous Egyptian Sphinx position.

"Hmmm... the King of the Jungle chasing a goat here or some Guinea fowl there. My, my, how the mighty have fallen, Charlie."

"Indeed, the diet changes and the desires subside but... the sun comes up in the morning and goes down at night. It's just the way it is, was and always will be," explained Charlie. "There is comfort, however small, in the order of things. I believe that it's called the circle of life." There was something quite regal about the old lion's philosophical tone.

"Well," started Jake as he rubbed his side against the granite rock, "that's easy for you to say, Charlie, because you're not being harassed, hunted and killed. I wonder how philosophical you would sound if someone from the East believed that hairs from your tail would cure the common cold?"

"What do you mean, Jake. Explain this to me?"

"Black rhinos, white rhinos, big, small, male, female and juvenile rhinos are being slaughtered. That's right, slaughtered for the so-called mystical qualities of their horns. All across Asia there is a belief that our horn has aphrodisiac and amazing healing properties. It's untrue, of course, but it wouldn't be the only untruth or fake news that has popular support."

The two beasts stared at each other. Bewildered by each other's isolation and yet, engrossed in each other's opinion.

"I hear you, Jake, but let's not forget that in 1910, Theodore Roosevelt, who was the President of the United States of America, journeyed all the way to Africa to kill a lion. Then, he had his photo taken with the dead King of the Jungle." Charlie coughed. Jake waited for him to stop.

"When we thought it couldn't get any worse, the dead lion was beheaded and skinned. These body parts were shipped back to America, where an overpaid taxidermist stuffed, treated and re-assembled the bits and pieces so that they might lie prostate on some games room floor!" More coughing. "All in all, Roosevelt and his son shot 512 animals! That total included 17 lions, three leopards, seven cheetahs, 11 black rhinos, and... a giraffe!"

He went on, "Lions are being groomed, fattened up and drugged so that the next filthy rich coward can enter the enclosure and shoot the Lion King. So, is it a testimony to his courage or, an endorsement of his shameful cowardice? Either way," continued the lion, "another one bites the dust." Once more, Charlemagne coughed and spluttered as Jake patiently watched.

"And so, Jake," the lion wheezed, "I'm not interested in your claim to being this great wildlife outrage. You are not! You are simply the *next* wildlife outrage."

Jake listened and found himself beginning to agree or, at least, understand.

"Whilst I still can, Jake, allow me to continue..." The old lion drew a deep breath. "Long before these poachers threatened you and your kind, leopards were being killed so that their coats could adorn the chest of the bass drummer in those marching bands. Still, before that," Charlemagne paused to emphasise, "the American Bison was shot almost to extinction for its meat, its hide and, how despicable is this, to actually starve the indigenous Americans, strangely called Indians! The bison were even shot at and killed for sport. Shot and killed from the luxury and comfort of chartered train rides!"

The old lion raised his scarred face and staring straight at the rhinoceros, asked, "Are you following this, Jake?"

"Yes."

"The Bengal tiger was shot onto the endangered species lists by Lord Dontgivashit sitting high in a basket atop an elephant!" More wheezing and coughing.

"Must I go on, Jake?!" challenged Charlie, regaining the roar in his voice.

The truth, wrapped in mutual respect claimed the silence.

"Don't you understand?" pleaded Charlemagne. "It just happens to be your turn on their what-shall-we-kill-next agenda. It's *your* turn, Jake!"

The rhinoceros stared at the lion. Even though he didn't look like it, the old lion spoke and sounded like the King of Beasts that he was.

"Oh! I understand, alright, I understand perfectly." He spoke slowly, picking the words that best suited his challenge. "You, Charlie, accept that you're on your way to death by, quote, the *order* of things, unquote. I, on the other hand, am on my way to the same place by the *disorder* of things. In spite of which, I am supposed to be as understanding as you? Well... that is not going to happen! Jake the

49

Black Rhinoceros will not go gently into that good night." He stamped his feet and tossed his head in that traditional two-step of his anger and defiance.

Unfazed by Jake's display, Charlemagne lowered his head, coughed into his beard and said quietly, "Oh, yes you will."

"What was that, Charlie? What did you say? I might not have good eyesight but I have excellent hearing," said Jake.

"Well, if your hearing is as good as you claim, you would have heard what I said. Repeating it will make neither of us right nor wrong, and besides, I don't want to leave on bad terms, Jake. Let's just say, we've both learned a lot from this chance meeting and we've both given each other something to think about."

Jake mellowed. "You're right, Charlie. I'm sorry for my outburst. I wish you well on your journey."

Charlemagne tilted his scarred head. "Thanks Jake, and may your journey bring you the answers you seek. Goodbye."

They brushed past each other as they continued on their separate ways. Probably to the same place?

Breakfast, Lunch and Supper

He didn't know how long he had slept. These days sleep and rest were the same thing. Jake always seemed to be listening. Every sound and noise had to be respected. Silence itches to be broken when you're nervous. Hardly anything can disrupt or deny rest like the sound you're expecting.

He liked being on his own. He had emptied his stomach, at last, and he became more alive to the things around him. Some rain had fallen during the night. Not one of those noisy thunderstorms when the rain hisses down from the darkened skies. No sudden flashes of jagged lightning. No, this was a gentle shower. The type that was gone as soon after it had washed all the dust from leaves that Jake now ate. The trees seemed to sparkle like the faces of freshly bathed children. Except for the pleasantly pungent smell that the earth releases into the air, there was hardly any other signs that there had been any rain at all!

Then, thought Jake, as the sun rises higher, the warmer air will take the aroma with it, and Jake knew that by mid-day, the last of the tell-tale 'bush smell' would vanish.

As he moved slowly out from the shade, he got the feeling that he was being watched. He stopped. Flicked his ears as he scanned the air to pick up any sounds. He heard light footsteps, perfectly placed and pointed like the dance of the cygnets in Swan Lake. He smiled to himself and watched un-noticed as the gazelles paraded, paused, passed and dipped their beautiful faces into the lush damp grass. Then, as if realizing their own beauty, they raised their heads slowly and gracefully to accept the applause of the birds atop a clump of thorn trees.

He stepped forward. The gazelles flickered into statue mode. Jake expected then to spring into life and exit stage left. They didn't. They just stared at him. Their beautiful coats twitched and shivered in anticipation.

"Good morning, ladies,' began Jake, "forgive my intrusion and please, just carry on as though I'm not here."

"Carry on what? We're just eating, and besides, you *are* here," said the prettiest one.

"Well, do you mind if I join you, then?" asked Jake, taking another couple of heavy steps towards them.

At that point, the small gathering *did* scatter, but very gracefully and not very far. Then, in unison they turned to look back at Jake.

Colours of light brown, beige, dark brown, white and black seemed to have fallen from heaven and landed gently and precisely on these most beautiful and delicate savannah ladies. The result? Elegance, grace, poise and charm.

"Whoa! Come back here," Jake instructed playfully. "I am a rhinoceros. Like the rest of my kind, I eat grass, plants and roots. I don't kill or hunt anything," Jake explained. "OK, I'll admit that when they were giving out beauty, you ladies were way ahead of me in the line. However, the difference between ruggedly handsome and butt ugly is a matter of opinion. So ladies, why not come back here and *change* your opinion?"

The prettiest one began to tiptoe towards him. Almost immediately, the other two followed her.

"That's better. My name is Jake. What's yours?"

"I'm Breakfast, this is Lunch," she turned her head toward the gazelle on her right, "and... this is Dinner," indicating the gazelle on her left.

Breakfast leaned forward, extended her long and graceful neck and, peering straight at him, said, "Boy, you are ugly. I mean, like, *seriously* ugly." Then, gathering herself, she added, "Oh! I mean that in the nicest possible way, though."

Lunch scowled at Breakfast. Whatever the circumstances, bad manners and rudeness cannot be tolerated. So, in an effort to restore Serengeti etiquette, she quickly added, "But I bet you're really clever and you've got a nice personality, hey Jake?"

"Well, ladies, let the facts tell their own story. I never notice my ugliness until someone points it out," explained Jake. "Anyway, ugly is OK as long as it remains on the outside. Which is exactly where I keep it. Out there for all, except me, to see."

"See," said Lunch, "I told you he had a nice personality!"

"He's also very smart and has good manners," chipped in Dinner.

"Enough is enough, ladies!" stammered Jake. "All these compliments are making me blush."

The gazelles lifted their heads, seemingly pleased with how they had deflected their beauty onto the rhinoceros.

"Pardon me for asking, but what are your horns for?"

"I don't know," said Breakfast. "I'm not sure that I've ever had to use them. Although, they do look rather nice, don't you think?" Not waiting to be corrected, she continued her haute couture monologue. "From the front, they are quite straight and perfectly positioned high on the forehead and yet, from the side, they sweep gently, and ever so slightly, back. In some cases, they may have a subtle upsweep at the tip. Some sort of tiara, perhaps?"

"Some sort of tiara, perhaps?" mimicked Dinner. "Well, I am sorry to bring reality to the show Miss Perfect, but your tiara, as you call it, won't make the slightest difference when Swifty the Cheetah is chasing your sweet tail across these grasslands!"

"Quite right!" emphasised Lunch. "You are not on Swifty's menu for your amazing good looks or your horns. Besides, how do think we got our names?"

All three began to giggle. A giggle which soon turned into laughter. Laughing at each other, laughing at what Lunch had said and laughing at Jake shaking his head in disbelief.

Then, on cue, a secretary bird strutted through the space between Jake and the gazelle. Head high, hooked beak, extended tail feathers, black leggings to just above the knee and those tell-tale quill feathers bobbing in unison from an invisible bun at the back of her head. "Secretary bird, indeed," mused Jake, "more like ballet mistress."

He was about to speak about *his* horn and then checked himself. He realised that nothing he could say would add to the moment. How could they all be so carefree, he wondered. He was feeling quite envious of their zest for life. They seemed to have no fear of death. They lived in the now, sprinkling it with innocence, laughter and stunning good looks. They all continued to joyfully nibble away at the Serengeti grass.

Suddenly, the ground tingled and trembled. Jake looked up. The gazelle were gone. They were gone so quickly it left Jake wondering whether he had actually seen them. Then, as if they were running across a painting, 80 or 90 Thomson's Gazelles dashed past. Some leaping to get ahead, or at least trying to avoid their brothers and sisters as they sped towards the emergency exit.

Through the dust, Jake could see why.

The cheetah was gaining fast and the herd of gazelle began to split into small groups. This seemed to confuse the young male cheetah. He checked his stride, changed direction and accelerated. Arching his back, extending his front legs and then gathering all four feet together. Then arching his back once more in nature's iconic explanation of sheer speed. It was hard for Jake to tell whether the gazelles were slowing down, or the cheetah was speeding up. One thing was certain, the gap between them was closing very, very quickly.

The small group of panic-stricken gazelles had scattered. Then, in the blink of an eye, it was one-on-one. Everything seemed to speed up! Left, then right, then left again. Suddenly and without even checking his stride, the cheetah swiped at the gazelle's trailing leg.

She tripped as her legs got all tangled up with each other. Her beautiful face smashed into the ground. There she was. Skidding along on her back in a cloud of dust and torn up grass. Before she came to a stop, the cheetah was on her and sunk his teeth into her throat. She kicked her hind legs just once and then lay still. Lifting his head and stretching his neck the cheetah dragged the gazelle slowly and gently and away. It all seemed so well choreographed.

While all this was happening, the rest of the herd had re-grouped and continued grazing barely 20 yards from where the scene had played out. Hmmm... thought Jake, just another lunch break out here on the plains of Serengeti.

The savannah is rich in grasses. The open country is scattered and splattered with trees that seem to be more excited about growing sideways rather than upwards. They appear to be about the same height. It's as though they had arrived at life's T-junction and simply spread out all ways from there. They are all happy trees. They don't compete for sunlight or water. They all get an equal share of whatever is on offer. Rain, wind, fire, drought and flood. Each gets its own portion.

There are some interesting names, too. Names like Strangle Fig, Sausage Tree, Candelabra, Baobab, Commiphora, and they all have a story to tell.

Jake smiled as he recalled the legend of the Baobab tree.

It seems that many, many years ago, long before Mohammed, Buddha, Moses and Jesus, the Great Spirit gave each animal a tree to plant. The Hyena was asked to plant the Baobab tree. Known for their carelessness and appalling table manners, Harvey's forefathers planted the Baobab tree upside down! Typical, thought Jake. So, that's why the branches of baobab look like bent and buckled roots. These castle-like guardians of the grasslands, sometimes appear to be as wide as they are tall. They are old. Very old. Some of them could be hundreds of years old and then, as if having seen it all, they simply break down, die and return to earth. Then... a seed sprouts and the next thousand-year-old baobab reaches up to the pale blue sky over Serengeti.

Jake looked up. A single yellow-billed kite was circling high overhead...

I Can See Forever...

He was sure he'd seen the bird before. In fact, even when he couldn't see it, he had the feeling that the bird could see him. He watched as the kite seemed suspended on the air. Just the tips of its wings and the flick of its forked tail gave any indication that this bird was actually moving. The cloudless sky denied Jake any reference point for the raptor's speed, height or direction.

"I bet he can see the whole world from up there," thought Jake. "I wonder if I looked down from where he is, would I still look like a black rhinoceros or, for that matter, a white rhinoceros?" Jake smiled at his own ignorance and continued marvelling at the kite in flight.

His daydream stopped. Wait. The kite folded its wings in tight against its body. The bird seemed to get longer as beak, body, legs, wings and tail squeezed themselves into an arrow-like shape. In an instant, this heavenly sentinel was accelerating out of its cloudless paradise towards the earth.

Just when it seemed that the yellow-billed kite would smash into the ground, his wings snapped open to where they belonged. His legs returned to their under-carriage position and this dark brown bird of prey skimmed across the top of the grass. Then, pulled up gently and landed just a few feet from Jake's snout.

"Hello, Jake!" screeched Billy. "How's life four foot above the ground?"

"I'm just fine, Billy. As if I haven't got enough problems, you nearly gave me a heart attack with that no-more-mister-nice-guy manoeuvre of yours!"

"I didn't mean to alarm you, Jake but I have to admit that it must look rather impressive from down here "

"How do you do that?" quizzed Jake. "One second you're Lord of the Skies and next minute you look like you've just been fired out of some kind of rocket launcher?"

"It's my party trick, Jake and it still gets a lot of attention. You know what I mean? It's like when you guys smash into a scout car and roll the Land Rover over!"

They both chuckled. "The old gags are still the best, eh, Billy?" And then, without altering his tone, Jake enquired, "Tell me, how long have you been following me?"

Billy did that nervous tick thing that all birds of prey do. His head twitched rather than moved. The neck feathers re-shuffled themselves. When stationary, his entire personality was about his head. The eyes, the hooked beak... Billy the yellow-billed kite.

"Four days," replied Billy. "Just one more to go, and," he paused, "for the record, I have not been *following* you. I've been *guiding* you. In fact," Billy continued, "you might say, *you've* been following *me*." The giggle had gone out of Billy's voice.

"One more to go? What does that mean?" puzzled Jake.

"Five minus four, equals one," replied Billy.

"Yes, I know that but what has that got to do with me?"

"Avi told me you've got five days to yourself and then... you've got to come back. She told me to keep an eye out for you and to make sure you didn't take a bath."

Jake dropped his head as his promise to Avril hit home.

"That's right, Billy. That's quite right; however, I have not finished thinking yet. So, tell Avi that I need more time."

"That's a lie, Jake! You *have* finished thinking. You just don't like what you're thinking about!' Billy hopped to the low hanging branch of a young toothbrush tree. The branch strained and bobbed under his weight.

"You buy in or, you bow out," continued Billy. "You cannot adjust time to suit the way you feel. This is now. To waste now is the first step towards lying to yourself." He paused.

"Asher, Charlie and the gazelles are all telling you the same thing, but you don't want to hear it. No, you just want it your way!"

He stepped down. The branch flicked back to its normal position and swayed up and down in its relief. Now, a yellow-billed kite on the ground looks a little clumsy. A sort of a hop, step and jump and always in the same direction.

From his new vantage point, and looking at his reflection in Jake's left eye, Billy continued, "Do you think that yours is the only well-being under threat?" Before Jake could answer, he went on, "Don't kid yourself, Jake. Us yellow-billed kites do not swoop on prey as much as we used to. No sir, we eat roadkill, scavenge in dustbins and some of us even hang around the city dump. It's a case of catch as catch can. Furthermore, it's quite likely that the next generation will not believe how we used to soar, dive, swoop, hunt and capture our daily bread." He blinked quickly as he allowed the memory to focus his point of view.

"Ask yourself, Jake. Ask yourself what do birds of prey prey on, when there is nothing left to prey on? You, more than most of us, will understand that the whole planet is feeling the pain of centuries of abuse." The kite hopped and one-flapped his way back to the skinny branch.

"We're all hurting. Our food is running out, their food is running out. The rivers don't know when, or if, the next rains will get here. The ground is heating up, the forests are being torn down, the skies are full of carbon gases and the food chain is missing too many links." Billy paused, then added solemnly, "The future is not what it used to be, my friend."

Then, as if to deny all that he had just said, Billy exploded, "I say, to hell with the future. All that matters is now!"

Billy paused long enough for Jake to ask, "Are you finished?"

"No!" screeched the kite as he dropped lightly back to the ground. "I'm just getting warmed up and you are very welcome to jump right in while I catch my breath?"

The silence suited both of them. Billy one-flapped back onto the toothbrush tree and bobbed up and down as the breeze tickled his feathers and played with the whippy branches. Jake could feel the self-same breeze gently strumming the hairs in his ears.

"So, what are you saying, Billy?" began Jake. "Are you saying that me and my kind should go hornless into extinction?"

"No. That's not what I'm saying," corrected the kite. "Furthermore, that is unlikely to happen." Billy began to calm down.

"What is most probable is that your numbers will continue to dwindle. They will dwindle until enough of them – human beings, that is – find a good enough reason to protect and preserve you. Then, it'll be zoos, game reserves, protected parks, farms, nature reserves, de-horning, museums, pink dye, 3D printers, safari parks and the like. Then, secondly..."

Billy stopped, twitched again, then turning his head away from Jake, he said , "Secondly... what is also highly likely, is that you will be killed before any of that comes to pass. Or, to be perfectly honest, Jake, you will be killed, soon."

The wind dropped and stillness stole the moment. Billy fluttered his wings, steadied himself on his skinny branch, and looked straight into Jake's face. "But I believe that you already know that."

"Well," began Jake, "I've certainly thought about that, Billy, Although, I'm uncomfortable with your use of the term, dwindle. Is that the same as systematic slaughter? C'mon, Mr Kite, don't sanitize this. I get your point, but..."

"But nothing, Jake! Listen, the poachers have seen you. They saw you when they killed Reuben. They know who you are. They know what you look like. They know where you live. Jeez, Jake, for crying out loud, they fired their guns at you! They are on your trail. They want you dead and they want your magnificent horn, or horns. They want them in their bag as they jog back to Somalia or, wherever..."

To Begin With

Jake turned for home. With Billy circling high overhead, he felt safe. He felt strangely calm and yet very aware. Not in a negative or insecure way, but aware of all that was good. It seemed that all that was good was all around him. Why is it that tragedy, fear and threat remind us to notice reality? He walked with his head up. He didn't shuffle. He walked sure footedly and with purpose.

It was mid-morning and the sun was beginning to heat things up. Jake eased his way into the mottled shade of a scrawny tree and rested. He was sure he could hear a scratching sound. Then, a faint sort of hissing... He stopped. Slowly turning his head toward the sounds, he stared then blinked his dull eyes into focus. Aha! Karl the Chameleon! Jake studied him with amusement. About six inches long, with eyes that could swivel and rotate independent of each other, a tongue that could extend to nearly twice the length of his body. Karl's tail seemed to have a mind of its own. One minute it was curled up in a spiral and the next minute extended to steady its slow-moving owner. Then there was his rough pre-historic looking skin, which could change colour to suit his surrounds in less than 25 seconds! Karl was Halloween on four legs. Good heavens, mused Jake, and they think *I'm* ugly!

Karl was the king of camouflage. He could change colour and hide in plain sight. His deliberate movements could mimic a leaf disturbed by the breeze, or pass him off as grey bark on any old tree. His feet, if you could call them that, appeared to operate more like tiny clamps. Everything about Karl was slow. His traditional name was *hambe gahli*. Which means go slowly, go safely. However, few things were as fast, or as accurate, as Karl's tongue! It all balances out, thought Jake, if you're that slow, however else are you going to catch your food? Isn't nature wonderful, thought Jake.

As he walked on, all the elements appeared to collaborate to show favour. The birds seem to assume the nature of angels and gently console him with their carolling. The far-off mountains, the rolling plains and friendly hills protect and inspire by just being there. It's called kindness.

The roots in their growth, the grass in its greenness, the leafy boughs and trees all make merry in their own way. Nameless flowers in their loveliness pour out their delicious fragrance and smile their best. The sunbeams, though tongue less, speak saving messages. Shady bushes rejoice to give shelter. In short, every living creature we see or hear gives us friendship, refreshment and comfort. Indeed, for all their silence, they tell of wonder. A wonder far greater than themselves.

He smiled, a full-grown black rhino with a spring in his step? You couldn't make it up!

He was surprised at how quickly he came upon his old stamping ground. Wasn't it always like that, though? The journey home seems quicker or shorter than the journey out? As he approached, two little heads popped up over the rim of the donga. Wild dogs, mused Jake. They're not wild, they're just hungry. Besides, if dogs are known as man's best friend, what's the 'wild' bit about? He preferred to call them 'painted dogs'. In fact, their Latin name translates to painted wolf and, just like Jake, their only predator threat came from humans.

"Kelvin! Is that you?" called out Jake.

The two puppy faces disappeared below the donga rim and slowly Kelvin emerged from the shallow end. His long legs made his walk look more like a lope. Somewhat sloppy and disinterested. That sixth-formers-bored-to-tears stroll. Kel's strong jaws gave away his meat-eating diet. His upright large bat-like ears suited his multi-coloured coat. Dark brown, ginger, white and black and a bushy tail with a white tip. If he was a cat, he'd be a calico. Rolled in mud but... a calico nonetheless.

"Good day, Jake, how is life treating you?"

"Oh, same as always, Kel. A little rain, a little sunshine, a bit of laughter, a few tears. Same old, same old," answered Jake. "And how are you?"

"I'm good, thanks. There's always hungry mouths to feed so, I'm kept busy." Kelvin paused. "I was sorry to hear about Reuben, Jake. I liked him."

"Thanks, Kel. It is a sad business and there's a lot of it going on."

Jake continued, "Seems Asher's lot are dwindling faster than they can breed. It's all about their ivory tusks. If you ask me, we'd all be better off if they were farmed and cared for."

"I agree, Jake, something has to be done. Poaching and trapping for the pot is what has gone on for centuries, but this tusk and horn business is out of control. The poachers have all the sophisticated communication tools like the smartphones and GPS devices. They are generally assured of getting what they planned. Which tells me that poaching is a modern, profitable industry. Mark my words, Jake, the hippos and the warthogs are next on the list."

Jake smiled. Kel understood. He was a family man. Caring for the young and old alike. Treating the sick with kindness and feeding and cleaning them.

There was no anger of bitterness in the pack; they all seemed to get along. Oh sure, a pack of 6 or more is a well drilled and efficient killing machine. It's generally a bloody and noisy affair. But that's life, dinner and death, out here.

"Are you coming to The Water Hole tonight, Kel?"

"I can't Jake, I got some little ones to look after. I'm sure Avril will fill me in later. Take care and good luck."

Jake had forgotten about Avril. It was nice to hear her name again. The sun was up, so he lazily strolled into the shade of a mature Balanite tree. He had a lot to think about and he was enjoying mulling it over. It's good to think about things. Not always reaching for the answer, just making friends with the facts. Striving to strip away the emotion that can so often distort things. He knew what he was going to do. He just needed to find a way to do it.

He must have dosed off.

"Jake, are you awake?" she whispered.

"Not yet, but your being here has got me working on it," came his yawnery reply.

"Jake, it's me, Avi. Are you awake?" she whispered a little louder.

"Hmmm... I'd like to say 'No'," quipped Jake, "but that would be a lie, wouldn't it?"

She hopped and stepped around his head and finally settled on the lesser horn halfway down his long snout between Jake's eyes.

"Welcome back, Jake!" greeted Avril. "Where did you go? Did you have a nice time? How was the weather? Did you see anyone I know?"

"Avi, you know exactly where I went and yes, everyone I met knew you, especially Billy."

"Oh, so he told you," said Avril behind a false surprise.

"He did, but don't worry, I'm not cross or anything. In fact, I'd like to thank you. It was very thoughtful of you to ask Billy to look out for me and very kind of him to do so."

Avril was somewhat taken aback by the gratitude and sincerity in Jake's voice. It sounded a little out of character. Oh, she knew he had a softer side, she just hadn't seen it in while.

"So... what's the plan, Jake? What are we going to do?" enquired the relieved and excited ox pecker.

"We?" said Jake. "We?"

"Well, you know what I mean, Jake."

Jake grinned. "Yes, Avi. I know what you mean but the 'we' now means everyone. It's no longer just you and me. It's everyone, everything, all of us."

Jake paused.

"Spread the word. I shall be at the water hole this evening. For those who want to hear, what I have to say."

The calmness in his voice was soothing and compelling.

"The waterhole?" queried Avi. "Not the Clearing?"

"The waterhole," confirmed Jake. "Yes, I know it's out in the open but we are going to need a lot of space if everyone pitches up."

"OK, Jake, but... you don't give me much time with this."

"That's right, Avi, I haven't given you much time because I don't have much time to give."

She nodded. Was this really Jake? Was this Jake the Black Rhino who less than a week back had scolded everyone with his foreboding, his insults and challenges? The same Jake who threatened the entire kingdom with his anger, sarcasm and contempt?

"Are you waiting for me to fire the starter's pistol? Get going, Avi!" ordered Jake.

She flapped, fluttered and was gone.

The Waterhole

There were a good number of impalas, wildebeest, zebra and giraffe already gathered at the waterhole. The sun was sinking low and Jake watched from just inside the treeline about 100 yards away. There is a stillness about the sunset out here. The sun's heat has made animals tired and thirsty. When that happens, there is harmony in the animal kingdom of Africa.

Even the dust looks tired as it floats around the hooves and smoulders among the legs of the early arrivals. There's always a little bit of nudging and bumping as the thirstier jostle for a place at the water's edge. The giraffe are given the most room. Long necks, long straddled legs and deep thirst take up more space than buffalo or warthog. The common thirst brings out the best in all creatures. It was their water and it belonged to all.

Jake started out towards the thirsty mass and at almost the same moment Asher, the bull elephant, approached from the opposite side. He and his entourage ambled purposefully to the water. When Asher was about 10 feet from the water's edge, he stopped. His head rolled from side to side. He extended his ears as he dipped and swayed his huge body. The dust gathered in a halo around him and then, he raised his trunk and trumpeted. He trumpeted again. This time, a lot louder.

The drinking stopped. Buffalo picked up their horny foreheads, the oxpeckers fluttered to new positions. The gazelle twitched and flickered. The zebras' coats trembled, shimmered and shivered. The giraffe stumbled upright. All eyes turned to Asher.

From across the cool, refreshing water, Jake nodded his greeting to Asher.

The elephant dipped his head in reply and said, "Jake has something to say. We should listen."

"Thank you, Asher, and thank you all for coming out this evening. I won't keep you long," began Jake.

"Firstly, I cannot apologize for *what* I said in the clearing last week but I am deeply sorry for the *way* I said it. My anger and grief got the better of me, and with your help, I shall try not to let that happen again."

There was a shuffling of feet and hooves from around the water as Jake's opening remark eased the tension.

Jake lifted his head and began to speak clearly and calmly. "Our lives, and deaths, are beyond our control. Our future, whatever you perceive that to be, is in the hands and hearts of human beings. That is a fact. We are among the inevitable casualties of their greed, their wickedness, their ignorance and their power." He paused.

"What do you suggest we do, Jake?" Asher asked.

"The only thing we *can* do," began Jake, "and that is... remain true to what we are."

"What the hell does that mean? 'True to what we are?' Is that Rhino-speak for grin and bear it? Come, come, Jake, tell it to us straight," Asher pleaded.

"Very well, this is what it means," started Jake. "Do what you've always done, only do it better. Fear not the future. Asher, you and your kind, are the biggest of all of us. Get dangerous again. Your strength is unmatched anywhere in the kingdom. It's who you are. If they want your tusks, let them know that it comes at a cost. Yes, they might still take your ivory but don't make it easy for them. Raise their level of risk. Increase the danger by being true to what you are. You are the biggest, the strongest, and the most powerful!"

There was a nodding of heads from all gathered.

"Asher," continued Jake, "your relationship with humanity is littered with stories of villages being smashed to the ground, trees uprooted, trackers trampled, hunters pierced through and safaris scattered. You have performed in their circus, worked in their lumber yards, marched on their parades and carried their royalty. They are in awe of your strength and your long memory. Keep them in awe!

"This poaching business brings them into our arena. They have to come to us to get what they want. Then, weighed down by their ill-gotten goods, they have to get back to their masters. The pay master, the yard master, the harbour master. Theirs is a long journey. They will be vulnerable. Keep it dangerous for them. Let them know that it is, *indeed,* a jungle out there! Our jungle!"

Asher lowered his head. He shuffled his front feet. Jake's words were hitting home. He gathered himself.

"Jake is right," began Asher. "Jake is right!" he said again. "Our glory is in what we are. They will find ways of looking after us because our real worth is not skins, horns or tusks. No! Our true worth is how we live side by side. It astounds them! We *are* our environment. Collectively, we hold the answers to so many of their questions. They have no need to go to Mars, Venus or Jupiter. What they seek is right here. Understanding us will unravel their future!"

Asher turned to Jake indicating for Jake to carry on...

"Our environment is getting smaller. Farms, mines and de-forestation are shrinking our Garden of Eden. We are expendable."

"I shall go to the mountain. Along the way I shall tell about what we have said and heard." He paused. "And yes, it is likely that I shall be killed but my spirit will not die." He drew a deep breath, scanned the outer edge of the waterhole and turning to the other listeners, Jake continued.

"Your spirit must not die. It must live on in the energy and effort of those who choose to care about us. Those who can and will protect us. Those who truly care about the environment!"

There was much murmuring, shifting and twitching. There were snorts, coughs and bellows. There was approval.

Then the dampened sound of paws in a hurry accompanied by quick rasping breaths, lolling tongues and dripping saliva.

"They're coming. There's two of them, Jake. They know you are here!" barked Kel the wild dog

"Quickly, Jake. Get in here." PJ, the zebra, opened a gap amongst his herd. Jake slipped alongside and the herd closed up.

The wildebeest folded around the zebra. Kel and his pack stood their ground as the Jake entourage moved off towards the trees. Asher and his lot tagged onto the vanguard and the gazelle scattered in every directionkicking up thick clouds of dust as they went. Through the dust, the outline of a young lioness could be seen. She was standing guard.

Issa, the poacher with gun, stopped. Hassaan, the poacher with the axe and the bag, stopped. Jake didn't.

The Journey...

It was morning and the savannah was busy. A symphony of sound serenaded the grasses and a slight breeze caused them to sway in a dance of delight and gratitude.

Jake's sharp hearing began to separate the sounds. The trill of hoopoe, the tap-tap of a hard-at-work woodpecker, the hurried giggle of francolin and the clumsy wing slap of disturbed guinea fowl. The savannah philharmonic was in perfect tune! Thoughts of how this journey would end were hidden in the joy of the now.

"Jake, are you smiling?" quizzed Avril.

"Yes," he replied, "I suppose you could call it that."

"Why?" Avril asked.

"Why?" mimicked Jake. "Why, do you ask. Didn't anybody tell you that the smile is that facial expression that has no explanation for, it has a *thousand* explanations? It is what it is, and therein lies its beauty and its mystery."

"Very well, then. Let me put it this way," Avi continued. "Why are you so clever?"

"No, Avi. I'm not really that clever," answered Jake. "However, when one is the latest version of a dynasty and species that has been around for approximately 350 million years, one picks up a lot of information along the way." He continued, enjoying the chance to sound as clever as Avi thought he was. "One adapts," he went on, "one changes, one fits in, one fails, and succeeds, one endures and eventually, one learns." Jake was in full flow and relishing his moment of unresearched philosophy. "The most important lesson is this," Jake spoke slowly; "you must *always* strive to understand! Understanding is the first step on the very long journey towards wisdom. As you know, Avi, wisdom is that cocktail of learning, experience, knowledge, strength, patience and courage." Avi didn't know, but to interrupt Jake at this stage would be an awful mistake. "This cocktail," continued Jake, "is stirred, not shaken, it is sipped slowly and reverently from the hourglass of life."

Half expecting a standing ovation, a 'bravo' or a chorus of encores, Jake paused. Then asked, "Are you following this, Avi, or am I boring you?"

"Both." The oxpecker smiled.

Farming for their Lives

It was early morning. Dew on the grass and shafts of sunlight sprinting across the plains. The morning chorus warming up in the dawn shadows and for that brief moment every living thing seems to stretch and yawn its welcome of the new day.

A dull thump. Then another. A scraping sound and then another thump.

"What's that, Avi?" asked Jake.

"I don't know," replied Avi.

"Well go and take a look. It came from just beyond those trees," ordered Jake rather anxiously.

Avi flapped away. No sooner had she gone, than she was back.

"Farmers," she said breathlessly. "Do you want a closer look?"

"Yes, let's go."

Jake parted the long grass and looked into the opening.

"You can go closer, Jake. They're farmers, not poachers."

"That might well be, Avi, but farmers are humans and so are poachers."

"Jake. You pose no threat to them. Like you said, you don't kill to eat. Besides, they eat vegetables, fruit and chicken and, what's more, you don't rustle their cattle. Go closer. Get a good look."

Jake inched forward. The thumping that he had heard was the sound of the hoe as it landed on the damp, reddish brown soil. It was swung by a woman wearing a bright orange headscarf, a yellow and mauve printed dress and what looked like a Tottenham Hotspur's track suit top. She was smiling. Smiling as she worked. Her teeth white against her dark skin. That rich blue-black colour of the people of East Africa. A few feet behind her was a younger woman using her hoe to scrape the soil back and allow the water to trickle and giggle its way among the young maize plants. The younger woman wasn't smiling. She was laughing!

"What's that enclosure over there?" asked Jake.

"I don't know," answered Avril. "I'll ask Billy."

"Is Billy here, too?"

"No," replied Avi, "he's up there." Avi chuckled at her smart-ass reply.

Billy's shadow crept over the enclosure. The chickens clucked and flapped as they threw themselves in panic against the wire net. The goats crowded against the wooden fence and the sheep couldn't care less.

The enclosure was well kept. The wooden fences were crude and yet well made. Roughly hued poles, lashed together with rope or string. Sometimes with wire and occasionally braided plastic bags bought from the local shop and carried here on the winds of ignorance.

Jake smiled. "What is it with the fences? Are they supposed to keep animals in or, keep animals out?" Truth is, he thought, unless they are patrolled and maintained they did neither or, did both, badly.

Billy had settled on top of a small bush. "What do you think, Jake?"

"I'm amazed, Billy. I didn't know they had it in them. I didn't know or, I'd forgotten, how at one with the land, humans can actually be."

"Yes," agreed Billy. "What always impresses me is that there is no waste and no excess."

"Hmmm..." mused Jake, "they learned that from us."

Billy twitched his approval.

"Changing the subject, for a moment, Jake. How long do you think it will take to get to the mountain?"

"I haven't really thought about it in terms of time, Billy. As long as we keep heading in the right direction, we'll eventually get there," answered Jake.

"Well, that's OK, then, because this journey is not a straight line, Jake," warned Billy. "We'll need to travel when it's safe, and hide when it's not. Truth be told. It's not *our* journey as much as it's *their* hunt."

"I understand, Billy."

"Let me try, again," started Billy twitching as he slowly spoke. "You will be shot, killed and de-horned just like Reuben and the others." Billy paused. "And there's nothing you, me or Avi can do about it."

"Billy!" Jake was becoming a little agitated. "We have had this conversation before and just like before, I understand. Trust me," repeated Jake. "I understand."

"I do trust you, Jake. Nonetheless, we must keep moving. We must stay ahead of Issa and Hassaan."

"Billy is right," added Avril.

"I agree with both of you," confirmed Jake. "Believe me, I know what I am doing and I do understand your concerns. I also promise that when the time is right, this will all make sense. Perfect sense not only to you, but to all who care."

Avril looked across at Billy, lowered her eyes and shook her head.

All things bright and beautiful

"What's that droning sound, Avi?"

Jake could hear a stop-start drone. Then, a voice. A bit crackly but very confident, a lady's voice was describing the savannah and its many residents.

"Today, we will probably see lion, buffalo, cheetah and... if we're very lucky, a leopard!"

Avril came flapping swiftly back from her reconnaissance flight, landed lightly on Jake's shoulders and explained: "The drone-ing sound is the noise from that highly modified Land Rover carrying six very excited tourists on safari." Catching her breath, she continued, "They're important people, Jake. These tourists take pictures, carry binoculars and wear clothing they can never wear anywhere else. They return home and make their friends jealous. Who, in turn, visit us the very next year and so it goes on. Most of them remain amazed by everything they see. There are others," continued Avi, "who are just here for the food, drink and sunshine."

"Not unlike us, eh, Avi? Just here for the food, drink and sunshine."

"Hmm... I hadn't thought of it like that before, Jake, but you make a valid point."

"OK, Avi, ssshhh for a second. I'm going to get a little closer? I'd like to hear what that young lady is saying."

"Go ahead, Jake. They're only carrying cameras, not guns," Avi encouraged.

Jake sidled up to an old baobab tree. Stood behind it, lifted his head and strained his ears to listen...

"...The Serengeti ecosystem is a geographical region located mainly in northern Tanzania and extends into south-western Kenya. It spans approximately 12,000 square miles. The Kenyan part of The Serengeti is known as Maasai Mara," began the safari guide.

"... The Serengeti boasts the largest terrestrial mammal migration on the planet and is listed as one of the Seven Natural Wonders of Africa.. That is 1.3 million wildebeest all moving together!"

"Psst, Jake," whispered Avi, "wouldn't it be better if wildebeest horn held the magic that yours is supposed to? There would certainly be enough to go round."

"Avi, there are times when your mouth gets the better of your brain. Don't you understand? The more rare the potion, the more power it's deemed to have. Just like we only need a drought to remind us of the value of water? Now, if you don't mind, I would really like to listen to the young lady!!"

"...the Serengeti is also renowned for its large lion population and is one of the best places to observe prides in their natural environment. Approximately 70 large mammal and 500 bird species are found here. This high diversity is a product of the diverse habitats, including riverine forests, swamps, kopjes, grassland and woodlands." She paused.

"... Elephants, wildebeests, gazelles, zebras, hippopotamus and buffalos are some of the large mammals in the region..."

"Yeah, yeah, yeah! All very interesting, young lady, but will we see a black Rhino today?" boomed a loud, disinterested voice from the last row of seats in the open sided Land Rover. The voice belonged to an overweight man wearing a large and garish floral shirt. The buttons on the shirt strained as the buttonholes gaped to keep his oversized gut from spilling out onto his bright blue shorts.

"The black rhino is a shy..."

"Shy shmy, here we go again!" interrupted the fat guy. "The big five are all here but guess what, ladies and gentlemen, we aren't gonna see 'em. No sir, they did not tell you that when they were taking the $10,000 out of your wallet. Did they?" provoked the boor-ish, uncomfortably hot and annoying fat guy.

He continued, "You'll see enough zebra to trigger an epileptic seizure, more giraffe than blades of grass and they'll even point out 20lbs of freshly dropped hippo shit but... the big five? The big five are all in Nairobi at that wildlife conference this weekend..."

"Quiet, Walt!" pleaded a middle-aged lady in a safari khaki T shirt topped with a wide brimmed straw hat. "You're embarrassing us and yourself."

"I'm embarrassing! You say *I'm* embarrassing!! Our guide is the one who's embarrassing. Dragging us out here under false pretences and acting as though seeing nothing is all included in the price!"

Jake eased away from his hiding place and strode proudly towards the Land Rover.

"Keep going until they see you, Jake," Avi egged him on.

Billy swooped low over the tarpaulin-draped Land Rover. Then again across the bonnet of the car, gathering everyone's interest and pulling their startled eyes towards Jake.

"Good heavens! Look at that!" exclaimed the normally calm tour guide.

"What? Where?" quizzed Walt the fat guy, fumbling for the binoculars hanging around his neck.

"Two o'clock. Fifty yards. Just in front of that old baobab tree."

The driver eased the vehicle over to the left, bringing it to a stop to give all six excited tourist a look at one of Africa's rarest sights.

"Black rhino," whispered the lady tour guide.

Jake stood still. Lifted his head and paused, and then turned away to the right.

"That's it, Jake. Give them the profile. Show them just how amazing you really are!" whispered Avi to herself.

"Oh! My God! He's magnificent. Look Walt, he is stunning!"

True amazement is nearly always followed by silence. Jake's appearance was no exception. The safari vehicle was dead quiet. The savannah breeze dropped. Avi stood still on Jake's humped shoulders and Billy ghosted overhead. Time stopped. Respect, admiration, humility and hope took control.

Then, it was gone.

Thunder clapped, lightning flashed and rain showered its approval as the curtain came down. The vehicle started up and the guide unfurled and tied the side covers into place. Jake turned away and walked back towards the trees as the Land Rover moved slowly away in the direction from which it had come.

Man made

Jake looked at the rising sunlight and thought 'Hmm, I've got that in my eyes most of the day'. He cautiously ambled clear of the two young trees that he had used for cover during the night. Avi twittered into his left ear, "Good morning, big fellow ... are you in a hurry this morning?"

"No, Avi, but I'm hoping to find something better to eat. Better than what has been available of late. The ground is hard and rocky."

Later on, when the sun had risen well above the distant low hills, Avi was busy again, worrying the inside of Jake's ears.

Jake was quiet for a while, as he stripped the few leaves and thorns from a twig and munched on it.

"Jake, you must have known," chirped Avi, "that food and water would become scarce when you persisted with this route?"

"Yes. I did know that. I'm not complaining," replied Jake with a bored grunt. "It's my feet that are doing the complaining."

They plodded along in an easterly direction in what was certainly unfamiliar country. Black Rhinos are territorial. Two square miles is all they need. So, this pilgrimage of Jake's was most unusual behaviour, indeed. For several days now they had left the savannah scrub and the landscape had taken on an open, almost treeless, rolling hill type of terrain. Neither Jake nor Avi could see that the distant horizon, lying directly in their path, was outlined by dark, craggy mountains.

Later, when Jake was weary by the day's trek, they approached the crest of a small rise. Suddenly Jake lowered his huge head and let out an angry snort!

The ground fell away sharply. Jake was caught off guard. He was standing at the edge of the Oldupai Gorge. A steep-sided ravine in the Great Rift Valley which stretches across East Africa. It is about 30 miles long. The diggings at Oldupai Gorge have achieved great advances of human knowledge.

"What do we know about this place, Avi?" enquired a still shaken Jake.

"Well," began the oxpecker. "As I understand it, the first early human species occupied Olduvai Gorge approximately 1.9 million years ago. About a million years after that, human beings actually stood up and then about 17,000 years ago, what we have come to call *homo sapiens* occupied this site."

"Homo sapiens? What, or who are they?" asked Jake.

"Homo sapiens is the latest version of human beings. Just like the farmers, tourists, game rangers, conservationists..."

"And poachers?" added Jake.

"Yes, and poachers," acknowledged Avi.

"This site is significant in showing the increasing developmental and social complexities in the earliest humans. Discoveries have revealed the production and use of stone tools. Prior to the use of tools, they found evidence of scavenging and hunting. This was highlighted by the presence of gnaw marks that predate cut marks and the ratio of meat versus plant material in the early human diet." Avi paused for effect and the chance to tease Jake with his own words. "So, big fella, are you following this?"

"Of course," Jake half lied, "I'm following it but I'm not at all sure that I'm understanding it."

"Stay with me, Jake, and all will be revealed..." Avi lowered her voice in a feeble attempt to sound mysterious.

"The collecting of tools and animal remains in a central area is evidence of developing social interaction and communal activity. All these factors indicate to an increase in cognitive capacities at the beginning of the transitioning to human form and behaviour."

"Or, misbehaviour?" challenged Jake.

"Oh! Really, Jake, have it your way." Avi was annoyed. "You ask me a question, I answer it. I answer as accurately as I can and then, you adjust what you've heard to suit your own bias and prejudice!"

"Well..." Jake tried to defend but Avi was not having any of it.

"You hear but you don't listen. Then, sometimes, you do listen but you don't understand. Then, when or if, you happen to understand, you don't believe!

You know what, Jake? You just might be more homo sapiens than you want to believe."

Jake laughed. "You're right, Avi. The most believable truth is the truth that makes you smile, giggle or laugh."

"OK, Jake," said Avi starting to giggle, "let's just say that in two million years humans have managed to stand up on their two legs!"

"Hmmm... that's no big deal, a baby giraffe born in the wilds manages to stand on four legs in 30 minutes!"

They were both laughing. Really laughing. It felt good.

They were still laughing when Billy swept into view. There was an urgency about his flight. No soaring, gliding or swooping dives. No. Billy's five feet wingspan beat the air with purpose.

Getting closer

B illy pulled up on the ground in front of them.

"We've got to go. Go now! Poachers! The same two as before. Head for those trees. Hurry."

Jake dashed off towards a small, defiant group of dead-or- dying trees thinking, 'there's no cover there'. All the same, he kept going as Billy had instructed. When he got to the trees, he was relieved to find that they were perched on the rim of a large donga with shallow sloping edges. The bottom of the donga was littered with bushes about four feet high. Jake half stumbled, half fell among the bushes.

Keeping still when you're tired and anxious brings its own challenges... like breathing.

After what seemed like ages, because time ticks very slowly when you can hear your skin creak, Jake heard voices. Angry voices. Then that droning sound of an approaching vehicle. Somehow this vehicle sounded as if it was in a hurry. The rise and fall of the revs as the Land Rover bumped along the uneven track sounded urgent. More shouting. Dogs barking. Orders, instructions, responses and enquiries all issued and answered in that noise known the world over as... confusion!

As the noises reined overhead, Jake was beginning to feel a bit more secure or, less involved. Whilst taking in his surroundings, he caught himself staring in amusement at a small black dung beetle. George the dung beetle was less than an inch long and intensely busy. It was only when the shadow of Jake's huge head passed over him, that he paused in his labour. George had managed to form a rough ball of elephant dung over twice his size! He was rolling his prize away by standing on his front legs and walking his four back legs. In this way, he was manoeuvring the ball of dung in a straight line. Almost like a truck being reversed up to a warehouse door.

Jake then noticed that a female beetle was watching George's progress with more than casual interest. George had prepared a secret hole in the ground and his plan was to deposit the ball into the hole. Gladys, for that was her name, would then join him inside, where they would eat the dung together. Mating would follow and then she would deposit her egg inside a second ball. Later, it would hatch out into a junior dung beetle, and so their world turns.

Jake was lost in amazement and wonder. He felt he was being watched. Returning to reality he found that Billy had landed on the stump of a burnt out tree and was looking quizzically at his 4000 lb friend.

"What?" offered Jake.

"Exactly," replied Billy, "what are you doing?"

"What I've been doing for too long, now, Billy. Running from death and growing tired of it. In my fatigue, and isolation, I have been watching George here," said Jake, indicating to the small and still busy beetle.

Jake noticed that Billy was eyeing George as if George would make a welcome snack!

"Whoa! Billy. Don't eat the little guy. George and his kind do a great job of fertilising the savannah. Let me explain," Jake continued.

"They take the dung underground where the roots of the grasses, shrubs and trees are, and the dung gives everything a real good boost and when the rains come we all get the benefit of good vegetation. Do you understand?"

"Who is your *all*, exactly, Jake? I don't eat grass or shrubs."

When Jake looked again, George the dung beetle was clamped firmly in Billy's beak.

"That's just the way it is, Jake. You eat grass and shrubs. Cheetahs and lions eat gazelle and I eat whatever takes my fancy. Right now? George is my fancy."

"What?" added Billy.

"Billy!" he yelled. "If I hear that's *just the way it is* once more. I promise, I shall use this horn for a lot more than self-protection!"

"Oh!" shot back Billy. "That's nice. Very nice! I'm your eye-in-the-sky, showing you this way from that, and to be more precise, I'm saving your baggy ass and now... I'm threatened by the very horn I'm helping to protect!"

Silence.

Then, they began to laugh. Isn't it odd how being tired can often help find the funny side of things? They were still giggling and chuckling when Avril settled on Jake's shoulder.

She hopped up on to his long forehead and began to explain what all the noise had been about.

It seems that the game ranger, in the helicopter, had spotted those same two poachers and radio-ed in to the anti-poaching unit on the ground. Three trained and well-armed game rangers, one Alsatian dog and her handler had sped out of their base camp across the scrub land towards the diggings.

Issa and Hassaan switched their attention from killing Jake to saving themselves. They split up. Issa made his rifle visible by carrying it on his shoulder. Hassaan took the axe out of its bag and he, too, exposed the tools of his trade in order to force the heli-borne ranger into making a decision. Chase the shooter or, the bag man? Confusion and doubt are effective weapons in both attack and defence.

"They've split up, Smithy! I have given grid reference of the last sighting to ground forces. We're low on fuel, so heading back to you."

"Roger. Copy that."

The helicopter whirred overhead. Paused, turned out left and headed back to base.

What next...?

Hassaan headed straight for the nearest kopje and waited. He and Issa had always arranged to rendezvous at the closest rocky granite outcrop if their hunt was disrupted. There was always enough shelter among the trees, shrubs and grasses that grew between the large granite boulders.

Issa had sprinted off to a clump of thorn trees. The flat canopy gave him some cover. The brief twilight announced the night and then, under cover of dark, he made his way to the kopje.

Breathlessly, he crawled into the gap. "Hassaan! Hassaan!" he called out low.

Then again, "Hassaan! Hassaan! Are you here?"

"Yes. I am here, Issa, in the next gap. Come towards the candelabra tree. You will see me."

Hassaan took the dates out of his bag, offered one to his companion and bit into one himself. They both chewed in quiet thankfulness.

"We will get him, Hassaan. He cannot move as quickly as we can. He will get tired and begin to make mistakes. Then... the horn is ours!"

"Yes, Issa, I understand and respect your hope. However, this rhino is special. We have tried to get him before and have failed. Getting close doesn't count. Since we killed that other one, it seems that this one is going somewhere. He is always on the move. That is not the normal way of the black rhino."

Issa ignored Hassaan's comments. He knew that the black rhinoceros was territorial and that he marked his territory with urine and dung. He also knew that the black rhinoceros was fiercely protective over his piece of ground and would fight whom and whatever he considered unwelcome.

"Hassaan," whispered Issa, "the only thing special about this one is his horn. It must be nearly three feet long!"

"Yes, Issa. I agree with you but... don't you find it amazing that this rhino has managed to keep it? We are not the only poachers interested in it and yet, there it is! Almost three feet in length and right where it has been since birth and... some people might say, that's exactly where it should remain?"

Silence.

Then, "My friend, I must tell you, I have a bad feeling about this one. Let's just leave him and go home."

"Shut up!" spat Issa. "Let us rest. Rest is a weapon. Rest clears the mind and re-energizes the body."

The poachers slept.

Mount Kilimanjaro, Uhuru!

"Jake," whispered Avi. "We must keep moving. They know where you are and how fast or slow you're travelling. So, once they work out where you're heading, they'll set an ambush."

"By the way," chipped in Billy, "where are we headed?"

"Mt. Kilimanjaro."

The three of them rested. It had been an eventful day. The evening chorus was warming up. Jake eased away to a small candelabra tree and soon the savannah was splattered with shadow as the moon began to rise. Hiding stars as it did so.

"He's not going to get to Kilimanjaro, Avi," whispered Billy.

"He knows that, Billy. He knows that better than you or I. However, we all need a goal, something to aim at and a good enough reason to get there. Now, I'm sure you'll agree, Billy, that the extinct volcano, that is Mt. Kilimanjaro, is as good a spec on the horizon as any and... and isn't dying the best reason of all?"

"Kilimanjaro stands alone," continued Avi. "It's Africa's tallest peak and the planet's tallest free-standing mountain. The summit is more than 19,000 ft above sea level and it is called Uhuru. In Swahili, Uhuru means freedom. Maybe that's what's on Jake's mind, freedom. Freedom from all the hurt, the pain, the anger, frustration and sadness. Freedom from the overcrowded and abused Earth."

"Or..." interrupted Billy, "perhaps Jake recognizes the similarity, and kinship, with Mt. Kilimanjaro?

"What do you mean?"

"Well... they're both big, lonely, powerful." Billy paused. "And the volcano is extinct..."

"Don't let's go there, Billy."

"Where? Kilimanjaro?"

"No, extinction."

Silence overtook them and they slept.

They set off very early the next morning. After a couple of hours of slow progress, Jake came wearily to a halt. His head hung low beneath his shoulders. He felt as though he had been travelling eastward for half of his life! He was tired of the daily routine of trudging onward, resting and eating in new places. The urgency of this pilgrimage was beginning to sag. His crusade was losing its purpose. Why hurry to your death? It will come to you. No need to rush the inevitable.

At least the weather was good and he so enjoyed the feel of the sun on his broad back. There was ample food, and a good variety at that. In truth, he was just tired and his body was weary from his long journey. "Don't overthink this, Jake," he mused, "you're just plain tired."

The grass rustled. He slowly turned to see the cause. There, in a clearing, smaller than Jake's shadow, an old encounter was playing out.

This fight between the cobra and the mongoose is a classic wildlife conflict. They don't go out hunting each other. They just seem to bump into one another. They keep their eyes fixed on each other. Neither is prepared to back down. The cobra takes up a defensive position in a coil with head raised. The plan being to draw the mongoose into its space and then attack with a long sweeping strike. The quick-moving mongoose jumps out of reach and will attack the snake from another direction before the snake can get back into a striking position. This in-and-out movement both tires and discourages the snake. Then... the mongoose will leap in close and sink its sharp teeth just behind the snake's head.

'Fools,' thought Jake turning aside and continuing on his way. 'That scrap always ends the same. At best, they both get hurt. At worst they both get killed. It would be a lot easier if they just stayed out of each other's way. But... that's just the way it is, I guess.' Jake chuckled at his surrender to that worn out expression.

Billy flew slowly in front of him as though he had read Jake's thought and... to remind him to keep moving.

Jake trudged on and a short time later he heard the familiar sound of elephant feeding. Branches were being torn down from a mature Camelthorn tree and eaten by a lone bull elephant.

Moving cautiously closer, Jake thought he recognised Dan. It's no secret that elephants and black rhinos have no patience with each other. Jake looked to find a way around the elephant. Like most animals, elephant do not like being interrupted when feeding.

"Avi," Jake whispered, "is there another way around this?"

"Let me take a look," replied Avi, and she flapped her way towards the elephant. In an instant Dan swung his great bulk around, irritated by this hitherto unseen intruder. He raised his massive head and with ears flapping wildly, he trumpeted his annoyance everywhere.

"Let's get out of here, Jake! This could end badly for everyone," yelled Avi.

Jake shuffled backwards. Dan kicked the ground with his front feet, sending clods of earth and debris flying. Rolling his head from side to side, Dan began to charge. Now, there's no way of knowing the difference between the mock charge or the real one. Jake wasn't staying to find out!

As he turned to move away, Jake noticed that Dan's rear right ankle was badly swollen. Blood had dried a dark brownish red and was caked around the cable that had cut deep into Dan's leg.

Snares and traps are set by a different type of poacher. Those who kill for food, not trophy horns. The food poachers trap, kill and slaughter animals to eat. Then, there are those poachers who trap the animals, kill them and sell the meat. They call it 'bush meat'. Either way, the result is the same. Wild animals are killed.

The snares do not discriminate. Buffalo, kudu, wild dogs, lion, elephant, wildebeest, zebra, leopard are just part of a long list of animals that die in excruciating pain. Bush meat is an industry. It's a growing industry without rules or regulations. Bush meat is illegal and it is widespread. 'But then,' thought Jake, 'so is hunger and starvation.'

He was pulled from his dark thoughts when Avi explained, "There's a river ahead, Jake, and we have to cross it."

The Crossing

Jake arrived at the river's edge. The water was flowing gently in the main stream but was quite still near the bank. Out in the middle of the river was a large sandbank. He could just make out three crocodiles, their mouths agape as they lay basking in the sun on their sandy paradise.

There was a loud splash barely a metre in front of Jake. He stepped back in surprise as the foam and spray cleared. Now, there is something threatening and dangerous about the appearance of a 14-foot-long Nile crocodile. It is believed that the crocodiles' bite can exert a force eight times more powerful than that of a great white shark!

"Don't try to cross here, Jake. The banks are steep, the water is deep and, let's face it, rhinos are not known for their swimming skills."

"Any ideas, Ray?"

"How much time, have you got, Jake?"

"Well... I'm in a terrible hurry, Ray, I have death chasing me and death waiting for me."

Ray grinned. "Very well. Let me put it to you this way," the crocodile began, slowly. "If you really want to cross here, me and four of my kind, will tear you to pieces before you get halfway to the other side. Y'see, as far as us crocodiles are concerned, you are just a hippo with a horn and... no swimming ability whatsoever, or," continued the crocodile, "as we say down here on the river–" Ray paused– "dinner time!"

Jake's heart sank.

"So, take me through your story, again, Jake, exactly how big of a hurry did say you were in?"

"Please, Horatius. Just look the other way this time?" Jake could hear himself beginning to plead. Begging was his next option.

"Sorry, Jacob," said Ray returning the formality, "you know how this works. This is what we do. This is how we eat. We're crocodiles, Jake, not the local ferry service. However," Ray continued, "I think I'm starting to understand your situation and here's what I'm prepared to do... Around the next bend about half a mile upstream, the river narrows down to about 30 feet across and shallows to less than two feet deep. You could cross quite easily there."

"Thanks Ray, I won't forget this favour," said Jake, grateful for not having to beg.

"Oh! By the way, Jake, if I were to get to the shallows before you, then, you will have the same problem that you have had trying to cross here." Ray grinned again.

"Ray! What kind of favour do you call that?" Jake asked angrily. He was agitated. He was tired.

"I didn't call it a favour, Jake. You did." With that, Ray slipped below the surface of the water. Gone.

"C'mon! Jake! Hurry! Faster!" yelled Avi.

Rhinos look rather funny when they trot. Almost like a two-man pantomime horse stomping across the stage as the audience squeal their Christmas delight. Now the reason for that comical gait is because rhinos walk, and run, on their toes. What looks like their knee, is actually their ankle.

"Not far to go, now!" encouraged Billy from overhead.

Running out of breath, Jake approached the narrow part of the river. The trees grew back from the river edge and the water trickled and chuckled over the rounded white stones. Jake slowed as he saw the welcome crossing. He was very tired from the enforced trot along the riverbank.

"Keep going!" screeched Billy, mindful of the crocodile's intentions to get to the crossing before Jake. "You can make it, Jake! Don't stop!"

Jake splashed, and crashed his way across. His wet skin gave him a two-tone look as his legs and tummy were shiny and clean, while his body and back were dull and dusty. He stopped exhausted on the opposite riverbank. He was so out of breath, he felt he might topple over. He steadied himself and stumbled wearily into the shade. He slumped down and lay quite still. He dozed off to the slowing rhythm of his recovering breath.

He rested and wasn't too annoyed when Avi whispered, "Jake, wake up, I want to show you something."

He got slowly to his feet and shuffled along with Avril perched on his shoulder giving directions and bobbing back and forth to the rise and fall of Jake's motion.

"There, Jake. It's straight ahead," whispered the oxpecker. "Kilimanjaro! Uhuru!"

Jake widened his eyes and looked as far as he could see. Not very far. He sighed.

Avi knew he couldn't see it. He knew, she knew, he couldn't see it. Belief and hope are comfortable bedfellows.

Watching

L eropit sat on the wooden bench, secure inside his well concealed observation post. His gaze, aided by the Government issued binoculars, swept the plains before him. Leropit Lesororo was dedicated to his work and after almost eight and a half years had achieved the rank of Game Ranger grade 2.

Although his eyes scoured the thorn scrub of his sector of responsibility, his mind was on the dog handlers' interview that he was to face in just seven weeks' time.

It was odd. By nature, and practice, the indigenous tribes of East Africa do not keep pets. Dogs are working dogs. The Malinois Alsatian was big, strong, intelligent and train-able. The success of all dog units whether they are tracker dogs, sniffer dogs or attack dogs is all about the relationship between dog and handler. Trust and confidence are the hoped-for result from good training. The dog and the handler will not knowingly put each other in danger. They operate as a unit. The handlers' commands are short, sharp and delivered at the same volume and in the same tone.

Leropit was looking forward to his interview. He saw how dog handlers were respected, admired and... better paid. He wanted some of that.

Suddenly his sight was drawn to the antics of a mature yellow billed kite. The raptor was swooping down in front of the observation hut, then soaring out of sight and swooping back across Leropit's line of sight. Wings outstretched; Billy's shadow cruised across the front of the observation hut. Soaring and swooping, Billy was distracting Leropit.

'Why is the bird doing this?' Leropit mused. 'There is always cause and purpose in wildlife behaviour so, what is going on? What am I missing, here?' Staring past the performing kite, his gaze picked up Jake's broad back as he moved out from the shadows of the small thicket of thorn bushes.

Hmmm... large, mature, black rhino! Thank you, Mr Kite. I see him.

Leropit lowered his binoculars and smiled. This area of the park had not seen black rhino for quite some time. He would make a special note in his report, as soon as his shift was over and he had been relieved by young Thomas. Leropit glanced at his watch: 11h20. Thomas would be another 40 minutes.

"Good," thought Leropit, "but why did this rhino leave good cover in the middle of the day and why is he trotting when it is so hot out here? Something is not right!"

Leropit expanded his view beyond Jake. Then he saw them...poachers!

"Delta 3 to Sunray Base. Are you reading me? Over."

The radio in the operations room crackled into life.

"Sunray Base to Delta 3. Reading you 5s. Over."

"Poachers on rhino spoor in Delta section. Over."

"Roger. Delta 3. Copy that. Over."

"Rhino moving north-east. Eight hundred yards from my locstat. RE562 DY376. Poachers are 200 yards further east and closing. Over."

"Roger, Delta section. Chopper 1, Rangers, dog plus handler are scrambled. Over."

"Copy that, Sunray. Out!"

Dave Smith was born in Lancashire, England. He trained with the Royal Air Force and the Royal Navy and served in Operation Desert Storm. He had seen action in Afghanistan. War weary, and after his marriage failed, Dave replied to an advert to fly helicopters for a wildlife trust in East Africa.

The thought of flying in blue sky above green grass counting elephants sounded like the perfect place to do what he loved... flying. It would also give him time and space to gather up the pieces of his life and start again.

There were six occupants in the helicopter. Not surprising as the Airbus AS350B3 is, indeed, a six-seater. Dave the pilot, two armed game Rangers, Teddy the dog and Peter, called Pato, Teddy's handler.

Dave was flying really low. The wheels of the helicopter skimming, and sometimes brushing, the tops of the taller trees.

"Chopper 1 to Delta 3: Are you reading me?"

"Delta 3 to Chopper 1: Reading you 4s. Over."

"Chopper 1 to Delta 3: We will be overhead your loc in 3 minutes. Update your situation. Over."

"Delta 3 to Chopper 1: Poachers are 100 yards to rhino target. They do not have rhino visual. Repeat. Poachers do not have rhino visual! Over."

"Chopper 1 to Delta 3: Copy that. Out!"

Dave Smith raised the nose and started to convert speed to height. He wanted to be at least 500 feet above the target to get a good view of both the rhino and the poachers. Dave turned slightly right to offset and give the rangers a better look. The horizon expanded rapidly as the helicopter climbed.

Issa and Hassaan heard the helicopter and stopped.

A shot. Jake felt it sting almost in the same moment that he heard it. A single shot from behind grazed his left leg high up in the thigh. Almost immediately a second shot rang out and with a heavy slap, the .375 bullet smashed into his left bum cheek. Jake began to fall as if to sit down.

"Don't drop. Jake! There are trees up ahead. Take cover there!" screamed Avi as she flapped free of Jake's shoulder.

He limped, shuffled and struggled forward to some longer grass and a small thicket of young trees set among a cluster of granite boulders.

He positioned himself to see from where the shots had come. The two men were less than a hundred yards away and they now broke into a slow jog, knowing that Jake was hit, wounded and slowing down.

Jake could hardly feel the sticky blood trickling down his leg but he could most definitely feel the pain. He tried to turn around but the injured leg wouldn't join the other three in his effort. He tried again and managed to prop himself against the bigger of the granite boulders. He took a deep breath and started to assess his situation.

Isn't it odd, he mused, "that the more you try to keep quiet, the louder your body sounded"? His heart was beating like a big bass drum, his stomach rumbled and gurgled like lava ready to blow. His breathing seemed to roar like the wind. His skin seemed to creak and groan. Was silence always this noisy?

Jake leaned on his injured leg, and to his amazement, it didn't feel painful. Truth is, he didn't feel anything. He shuffled his feet into place and this time, all four moved into their proper positions.

Phew, that's a relief, thought Jake. I'm going to need all four legs to do their job when these poachers get close.

The charge of a black rhino is short and accurate. There is no U-turn.

The long grass worked out for all involved. As the poachers leaned into their jog the grass was as high as their heads. That same grass covered Jake. The poachers would easily see the blood speckled grass trampled underfoot as the wounded rhinoceros had hobbled and dragged himself to cover. As long as the poachers kept their eyes fixed on the spoor and blood trail, they would be unwittingly drawn into Jake's ambush.

The poachers stopped about 40 feet away. Jake thought that they had seen him. Then he heard it. The unmistakable sound of an approaching helicopter. Out on the plains, all sounds attract attention. Man-made mechanical noises are foreign, somewhat rhythmic and loud! Helicopters do not, and cannot, sneak up on a situation. As they approach a landing zone, the large rotor shakes the trees, bends and flattens the grass and hurls dust, dirt, rocks and stones into the air.

Whup-whup-whup the rotor smacks the sky and the flying dust and debris make visibility difficult and damned nigh impossible. Yes, helicopters land in a cloud of dust and a cacophony of noise to the applause of the ensuing confusion.

Issa panicked. Partly blinded by the swirling dust, he aimed in the general direction of the helicopter and fired. Hassaan the bagman was frozen in fear.

Jake rushed forward. By the time that Hassaan saw him, it was too late. Jake crashed into him. The horn tore deep into Hassaan's chest. Jake rammed the poacher against the granite boulder. Again, and again and again. Then, shook himself free of Hassaan's lifeless body and in doing so, the poacher's empty bag hung from his horn like a candy wrapper on a park ranger's spike.

The helicopter hovered about four feet above the ground. The Rangers, Teddy the dog and Pato jumped out into the dust and scattering stones. Issa fired another shot in the general direction of the chopper as it hovered upwards.

Jake charged. Pulling his head up on contact, he tossed Issa into the air. The gun sent spinning off in one direction as Issa crashed to the ground. Jake drove his horn into the gunman, ripping open his thigh. Issa screamed. Nobody heard him. Nobody cared. Exhausted, Jake tumbled forward, crushing Issa under his enormous chest.

Breath was scarce. Breathing erratic.

"This should not be happening," wheezed Jake.

"I didn't know you could speak!" gasped a startled Issa.

"I was sure you weren't listening..." said Jake.

Silence.

From overhead

It's a peculiar sight. A helicopter on the ground looks incapable of flying, thought Billy. It's as though the sky has to strain to get it into the air and the helicopter staining even harder to stay on the ground. Then, when this tug o' war stalls, the helicopter raises its tail, moves forward and then upward.

As if to show how flying should be done, Billy swooped low over this odd tableau of rhino, poacher, ranger, dog and helicopter and settled on a nearby thorn tree.

Avi flapped her way into the branches of the same tree. "What happened, Billy? What's going on? Is Jake dead?"

"I'm not sure, Avi," replied Billy. "There's a lot going on down there. I saw one dead poacher. There are two rangers with rifles and a third with a dog. Jake is down and... I think the other poacher is pinned under him."

Jake made as if to lift his head but it was too heavy and it flopped down onto the ground again.

"Hey!" yelled Pato the dog handler. "The rhino is alive!"

"What?! That can't be! He's got four bullet holes in him," called Ranger 1.

"No, he doesn't. He has two entry wounds and two exit wounds. I think the bullets went straight through. They missed the bones but may have nicked some of the vitals. Radio the base and get the vet here. Quick!"

Dave Smith flew back to the base on his own. It was a quick flight. Just 12 minutes to touch down. The vet would be ready with all his gear at the landing zone. It would be a touch-and-go landing and take off. Smith would keep the motor running and he would be back at the stricken rhino just 25 minutes after leaving him wounded, but breathing.

Mike Roberts was a veterinary surgeon. After qualifying from Onderstepoort in South Africa, he joined his father's practice in Sandton, a very well-to-do suburb of Johannesburg. Two years later and bored with rabbits, goldfish, parrakeets, expensive dogs and overweight pussy cats, he took a position with the anti-poaching unit in the famous Kruger

National Park. He learned a lot. When he was passed over for the top job, he applied for a job with the Kenya Wildlife Service. He got it. He loved it. He married Vanessa, a beautiful tour guide, and he was very, very good at this type of work.

The Airbus AS350B3 nestled on the flat ground about 50 yards from where Jake lay. He was awake and agitated. He couldn't move and when he tried, it hurt. A loud pop, like a champagne cork, rang in his ears. He felt drowsy. It went dark. Jake was tranquilized and a black bag had been placed over his head.

Mike Roberts went to work, quickly. Pato the dog handler was right. The rifle shots had, indeed, passed right through Jake's upper leg and bum cheek. There was no bone damage, but the muscles had been torn. It would be a long road back to full recovery.

"OK, gentlemen. This rhino will live. This black rhino will keep his magnificent horn! All we have to do, now, is get a recovery vehicle to transport him to the sanctuary. OK, everybody. Let's move. Let's move quickly!"

Billy turned slowly to look at Avi. She stared into his powerful face. After a prolonged silence, a rather embarrassed Billy twitched. "What?" he asked a bit awkwardly.

"Oh, is my favourite yellow-billed kite crying or... laughing?" asked Avi through a pinched smile.

"Both," replied Billy.

BVPRI - #0001 - 230822 - C0 - 210/148/8 - PB - 9781915338129 - Matt Lamination